HOME

SHIPMENT 5

The Texan's Baby by Donna Alward
Not Just a Cowboy by Caro Carson
Cowboy in the Making by Julie Benson
The Renegade Rancher by Angi Morgan
A Family for Tyler by Angel Smits
The Prodigal Cowboy by Kathleen Eagle

SHIPMENT 6

The Rodeo Man's Daughter by Barbara White Daille
His Texas Wildflower by Stella Bagwell
The Cowboy SEAL by Laura Marie Altom
Montana Sheriff by Marie Ferrarella
A Ranch to Keep by Claire McEwen
A Cowboy's Pride by Pamela Britton
Cowboy Under Siege by Gail Barrett

SHIPMENT 7

Reuniting with the Rancher by Rachel Lee
Rodeo Dreams by Sarah M. Anderson
Beau: Cowboy Protector by Marin Thomas
Texas Stakeout by Virna DePaul
Big City Cowboy by Julie Benson
Remember Me, Cowboy by C.J. Carmichael

SHIPMENT 8

Roping the Rancher by Julie Benson
In a Cowboy's Arms by Rebecca Winters
How to Lasso a Cowboy by Christine Wenger
Betting on the Cowboy by Kathleen O'Brien
Her Cowboy's Christmas Wish by Cathy McDavid
A Kiss on Crimson Ranch by Michelle Major

HOME *on the* RANCH

A TEXAN ON HER DOORSTEP

———— ⚒ ————

USA TODAY BESTSELLING AUTHOR

STELLA BAGWELL

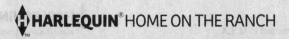
HARLEQUIN® HOME ON THE RANCH

ISBN-13: 978-1-335-45302-0

A Texan on Her Doorstep

Copyright © 2009 by Stella Bagwell

Printed in U.S.A.

www.Harlequin.com

After writing more than eighty books for Harlequin, **Stella Bagwell** still finds it exciting to create new stories and bring her characters to life. She loves all things Western and has been married to her own real cowboy for forty-four years. Living on the south Texas coast, she also enjoys being outdoors and helping her husband care for the horses, cats and dog that call their small ranch home. The couple has one son, who teaches high school mathematics and is also an athletic director. Stella loves hearing from readers. They can contact her at stellabagwell@gmail.com.

Prologue

The worn, yellowed envelopes bound with twine had been placed on Phineas McCleod's kitchen table more than an hour ago; yet he'd not touched them. Nor had his brother, Ripp. Both men had skirted around the stack of papers as though they were a coiled rattlesnake.

For the past several months, Mac, the nickname everyone called Phineas, and Ripp had searched for any trail of their mother, Frankie, who'd walked out on the family nearly thirty years ago. And up until yesterday, when Oscar Andrews, an old family acquaintance of the McCleods, had appeared on Ripp's doorstep with letters addressed to his late mother, Betty Jo, their searching had gone in vain.

Now, because of the letters exchanged between Betty Jo and Frankie, the brothers had more than clues. They had an address, a definite place to look for Frankie McCleod. Yet strangely neither of them was eager to race to the spot or even read the letters. Doubts about the search for her had settled like silt in the bottom of a wash pan.

Now, as Mac roamed aimlessly around his modest kitchen, he glanced over at his younger brother. Since Ripp had arrived an hour ago, he'd done little more than stare out the window. Obviously, learning about the existence of Frankie's letters had shaken him. Hell, it had done more than shake Mac; it had practically knocked him to his knees. Two deputy sheriffs, who'd faced all sorts of danger, were now jolted by the idea of seeing a woman who had been out of their lives for twenty-nine years.

"One of us has to go to this ranch and meet with her, Ripp, and it should be me," Mac said. "You have a family now. A wife, a son and a baby daughter. They need you at home. I don't have anything to hold me here, except my job. And Sheriff Nichols will give me time off. Hell, I've got so much sick leave coming to me I could take off a year and still not use it all up."

Ripp's snort was meant to sound humorous, but it fell a bit short. "That's because you're too mean to get sick." His expression dry, he looked over his shoulder at Mac. "But who knows—after this you just might need a good doctor."

Ripp didn't have to explain that "this" meant finding Frankie McCleod. After all this time without her, Mac couldn't think of the woman as their mother. Not in the regular sense of the word.

Mac said, "Well, we both decided after Sheriff Travers told you that story about Frankie calling Dad, asking to come home, that maybe we should try to find her. See if his story was true and what really happened back then. Are you having second thoughts?"

Groaning, Ripp turned away from the window. "Hell yes! I keep thinking that maybe not knowing about her is better than learning that she really *didn't* want us."

Mac thrust a hand through his dark hair as he stared at the stack of letters. Each one had been written by Frankie Cantrell and mailed to Betty Jo Andrews, who'd lived in

Goliad County all her life until she'd died three months ago from a massive stroke. Her son, Oscar, had been going through her things, getting her estate in order, when he'd discovered the letters in an old cedar chest. Frankie's last name had changed from McCleod to Cantrell, but Oscar had glanced through one of the letters and spotted Mac's and Ripp's names. As a result, he'd thought the brothers would be interested to see them.

Interested? The existence of the letters had stunned them. Betty Jo had certainly kept her correspondence with Frankie a deep secret. If anyone else had known about it, they'd not disclosed it to Mac or Ripp.

"I don't agree," Mac finally replied. "The not knowing is bad, Ripp. Besides, if it turns out she didn't want us, then it will be easy for me to say good riddance and put the matter out of my mind once and for all."

"That's cold."

Mac let out a long breath. "I can't help it, Ripp. I remember watching her pack up and drive away. That does something to a ten-year-old kid."

Walking across the room, Ripp placed a comforting hand on his brother's strong shoulder. "We don't have to do this, Mac.

We'll always have each other. If that's enough for you, then it's enough for me."

Mac's throat tightened as he looked in his brother's eyes. While growing up, the two had clung to each other more than most siblings. And down through the years that closeness hadn't wavered. Mac didn't have to think twice about his brother's love. Ripp would always be there for him, no matter who or what came and went in their lives.

"We both deserve to know the truth, Ripp. And I'm gonna find it." Mac gestured to the letters. "I'll take one of those with me for evidence. You can read the rest while I'm gone."

Ripp shook his head. "We'll read them together. Once you get back."

"We might not want to read them then," Mac countered soberly.

"Find the woman first, Mac. And then we'll make a decision about her."

Chapter One

"Dr. Sanders, if you have a moment could you come to the nurses' station? There's—someone here who I think you need to see."

Ileana Sanders frowned slightly. It wasn't like Renae to sound evasive. In the few years that Ileana had known her, she'd been an excellent nurse who didn't waste time playing guessing games.

"I'm working on a chart, Renae. Who is it? Do they need medical attention?"

"No. He—looks pretty healthy to me." There was a pause on the phone, and when Renae's voice returned, Ileana could barely hear her whisper. "Get down here now, Doc.

If you don't, I'm not sure I can keep him out of Ms. Cantrell's room!"

"I'll be right there."

Dropping the phone back in its cradle, Ileana grabbed a white lab coat from the back of her chair and left the little cubicle she used as an office while making her hospital rounds.

From the internal medicine wing of the building, Ileana had to walk down a long, wide corridor, then make a left turn and walk half that distance again to reach the nurses' station.

Along the way, she met several of the more mobile patients walking the hallway. They all spoke to her, and she gave each one an encouraging smile and a thumbs-up on their progress. One of the perks of working in a smaller town, she thought, was knowing most everyone who walked through the hospital doors.

But the moment Ileana turned the corner and peered toward the nurses' station, she definitely didn't recognize the tall man standing at the counter. Even though it was exceptionally cold outside, he was without a jacket, making it possible for her to see that he was dressed all in blue denim. A chocolate-brown cowboy hat was slanted low over his forehead and covered hair a shade darker than the felt. And in spite of the lengthy distance, she could see he was a walking mass of lean, hard muscle.

He must have heard the hurried click of her heels on the shiny tile, because he suddenly turned in her direction, and for one brief moment, Ileana felt her breath catch, her heart jump. His features were chiseled perfection, his skin burned brown by the sun. Authority was stamped all over him, and she knew, without being told, that he was a stranger to Ruidoso. There was a subtle edginess about him that was different from the locals.

Instinctively, Ileana's steps slowed as she tried to regain her composure, while to her left, Renae swiftly walked from behind the counter to intercept her.

"Dr. Sanders, this is Mr. McCleod. He's traveled all the way from Texas to see Ms. Cantrell."

His dark brown eyes were sliding over Ileana with a lazy interest that left her uncomfortably hot beneath her lab coat; yet she did her best to appear cool and collected as she stepped up to the man and thrust out her hand.

"Nice to meet you, Mr. McCleod," she said with a faint smile.

His big hand closed around hers, and Ileana was acutely aware of warm, calloused skin and firm pressure from his fingers.

"Call me Mac," he said. "Are you Ms. Cantrell's attending physician?"

The easy smile on his face was a tad sexy and a whole lot charming. As Ileana drew in a deep breath, she realized she'd never met this man. Because he was clearly unforgettable.

Inclining her head, she hoped she didn't look as awed as she felt. Which was really a quite ridiculous reaction on her part. She'd lived on the Bar M Ranch all her life. She'd been around rugged men throughout her thirty-eight years, and some of them had been darn good-looking with plenty of rough sex appeal. Yet none of them had grabbed her attention like this one. This was one striking cowboy.

"Yes, I'm Ms. Cantrell's doctor. Are you a friend of hers?"

Beneath his dark tan, she watched a hint of red color work its way up his throat and over his face. His embarrassed reaction wasn't the norm, but Ileana had certainly contended with worse. Everyone reacted differently when a friend or loved one became ill. Some got downright angry, quick to blame the doctor, even God, for the misfortune. She'd learned to take it all in stride.

The aim of his brown gaze landed somewhere near her feet rather than on her face, making her curiosity about the man go up another notch.

"Uh—not exactly," he said.

His face lifted, and Ileana couldn't help but notice the faint, challenging thrust of his chin, the resolution in his eyes. She shivered inwardly. For all his smooth manners, she instinctively sensed Mac McCleod had a very tough side to him.

"Nurse Walker tells me you're not allowing Ms. Cantrell to have visitors right now."

"That's right," she said, then feeling she needed to keep their conversation private, Ileana touched a hand to his arm and gestured to a waiting area several feet away from the nurses' station. "Why don't we step over here, and I'll explain."

He didn't say anything as he followed her over to a small grouping of armchairs and couches covered in green and red fabric, but once they stood facing each other, he didn't wait for her to speak.

"Look, Dr. Sanders, I've traveled a considerable distance to see Ms. Cantrell. At the

Chaparral Ranch, I was told by a maid who answered the door that she was hospitalized, so I drove straight here. All I'm asking is a few short minutes with the woman. Surely that couldn't hurt," he added with a persuasive little smile.

Even though he seemed pleasant enough, there was something about the way he said "the woman" that left Ileana uneasy. Besides sounding a bit disrespectful, there was no warmth, no fondness inflected in the words. Had he and Frankie had a falling-out over something? Did he actually know her?

"I'm very sorry, Mr. McCleod. Perhaps you should have called before you made the long drive. Ms. Cantrell isn't up for visits. Presently, her condition is very fragile. The only people I'm allowing into her room are her son, daughter and father-in-law."

For one brief moment his jaw hardened, but just as quickly a smile transformed his face, and Ileana felt certain he was deliberately trying to charm her into letting him enter Frankie's room. The idea was very odd and even more worrisome.

"What about her husband?" he asked.

This brought Ileana's brows up. Clearly he wasn't a close acquaintance of Frankie's. Otherwise, he would have known that Lewis, her husband, had passed away a little more than a year ago.

"I'm sorry if you didn't know. Ms. Cantrell is a widow now. Lewis died about a year ago."

His expression suddenly turned uncomfortable, and Ileana was relieved to see that the man did have a streak of compassion in him.

"Uh—sorry. No, I didn't know."

"Have you spoken with Quint or Alexa, Ms. Cantrell's children? Perhaps they can help you," she said.

Quint and Alexa. Mac mulled the two names over in his mind. If Frankie Cantrell was Mac's missing mother, and from every indication it appeared that she was, that would make Quint and Alexa his half siblings. The idea knocked him for a loop. For some reason all these years, he'd never considered the idea of Frankie having more children. A stupid, infantile idea to cling to, he supposed. But if she'd not wanted to be a mother to Mac and Ripp, why would she have had more children?

"No. I've not spoken to either of them," he told her. "I—I'm not sure there were any family members at home when I visited the ranch."

"Well, both of Frankie's children have

their hands full with trying to watch over their mother and keep up with their jobs, too. Alexa works in Santa Fe at the state capitol, and Quint runs the ranch here in Ruidoso. I expect he'll be around later tonight. If you'd like to wait. Or contact Abe Cantrell, her father-in-law."

Frustration made him want to howl, but he kept the reaction to himself. This woman wouldn't understand. And frankly, she was looking at him as though he were one of those criminals he often locked behind bars. Which was a strange reaction for Mac, who was used to women sidling up to him with a warm, inviting smile on their faces. He liked to flirt but hadn't gotten serious in a long time.

Hell, Mac, she's a professional. She isn't going to be flashing you a sexy smile or flirting with you.

She was a doctor. And from the looks of her, she'd never heard the words *sex* or *glamour*. She was plainer than vanilla yogurt and appeared to be one step away from a convent.

Except for a pair of deep blue eyes and naturally pink lips, her round face was pale and devoid of any color. Dark, reddish-brown hair was brushed tightly back from her forehead and fastened in a long ponytail at her nape.

The starched stiff lab coat hid her clothing, along with the shape of her body. Even so, Mac sensed she was as slender as a stick and as fragile as the petal of an orchid.

"I'm not sure I can wait," he told her. "You see, I was planning on talking to Ms. Cantrell about an—urgent matter." Besides, Mac wasn't ready to meet the man who might be his half brother. He'd only arrived in Ruidoso, New Mexico, a few hours ago. He'd driven straight out to the Chaparral Ranch in hopes of finding Frankie and putting the whole matter of her disappearance to rest. Now it looked as though there wasn't going to be any meeting or answers of any sort.

Dr. Sanders—Ileana, he'd heard the nurse call her— shook her head. "I'm sorry," she said again. "But I'm only allowing family members to enter Ms. Cantrell's room and even they are only allowed five minutes with her."

"Is she in the intensive care unit?"

The woman's shoulders drew back, as though remembering privacy laws for patients. He wondered just how well this doctor knew the woman. Maybe Frankie had been a patient of hers for a long time, but that didn't necessarily mean Dr. Sanders knew all that much about Frankie's personal life.

"Not exactly. She's in a room where she's monitored more closely than a regular room. That's why I made the decision to limit her visitors to relatives only. People can be well meaning, but they don't realize how exhausting talking can be to someone who's ill."

Mac's visit hadn't meant to be well meaning or anything close to it. Maybe that made him a hard-nosed bastard, but then in his eyes, Frankie had been more than callous when she'd walked out of Mac's and Ripp's lives. She'd promised to come back, but that promise had never been kept. Two little boys, ages eight and ten, had not understood how their mother could leave them behind. And now that they were grown men, ages thirty-seven and thirty-nine, they still couldn't understand how she could have been so indifferent to her own flesh and blood.

Mac's gaze settled on the doctor's face, and Frankie McCleod was suddenly forgotten. Plain or not, there was something about Ileana Sanders's soft lips, something about the dark blue pools of her eyes that got to him. Like a quiet, stark desert at sunset, she pulled at a soft spot inside him. Before he realized what he was doing, his glance dropped to her left hand.

No ring or any sign of where one had once been. Apparently she was single. But then, he should have known that without looking for a ring. She had an innocent, almost shy demeanor about her, as though no man had ever woken her or touched her in any way.

Hell, Mac, her sex life or lack of one has nothing to do with you. Plain Janes weren't his style. He liked outgoing, talkative girls who weren't afraid to show a little leg or cleavage and drink a beer from a barstool.

Yeah. Like Brenna, he thought dourly. She'd showed him all that and more during their brief, volatile marriage. Since then he stuck to women who knew the score.

Sucking in a deep breath, he tried again. "I guess you'd say I'm more than a visitor, Dr. Sanders. I—well—you might consider me…a relative."

Even if Renae hadn't told her that the man was from Texas she would have guessed. Not just from the casual arrogance in the way he carried himself, but the faint drawl and drop of the *g* at the end of his words were a dead giveaway.

"Oh? I didn't realize Frankie had relatives living in Texas."

"We haven't been together—as a family—in a long time. And we just learned that she was living in New Mexico."

Totally confused now, Ileana gestured to one of the couches. "Let's have a seat, Mr. McCleod. And then maybe you can better explain why you're here in Ruidoso."

Without waiting for his compliance, Ileana walked over and took a seat. Thankfully, he followed and seated himself on the same couch, a polite distance away.

As he stretched out his legs, her gaze caught sight of his hands smoothing the top of his thighs. Like the rest of him, they were big and brown, the fingers long and lean. There was no wedding ring, but then Ileana had already marked the man single in her mind. She doubted any woman had or ever could tame him. He looked like a maverick and then some.

With a sigh she tried to disguise as a cough, she turned toward him and said, "Okay. Maybe you'd better tell me a little about yourself and your connection to Frankie. None of this is making sense to me."

He glanced over to a wall of plate glass.

Snow was piled against the curbs and beneath the shade of the trees and shrubs. It was as cold as hell here in the mountains, and being in this hospital made Mac feel even colder. At the moment, South Texas felt like a world away.

"I imagine right about now you're thinking I'm some sort of nutcase. But I'm actually a deputy sheriff from Bee County, Texas. And I have a brother, Ripp, who's a deputy, too, over in Goliad County."

Ileana inclined her head to let him know that she understood. "So you're both Texas lawmen who work in different counties."

"That's right. So was our father, Owen. But he's been dead for several years now."

"I'm sorry to hear that. And your mother?"

His gaze flickered away from hers. "We're not certain. You see, my brother and I think Frankie Cantrell is our mother."

If a tornado had roared through the hospital lobby, Ileana couldn't have been more shocked, and she struggled to keep her mouth from falling open.

"Your mother! Is this some sort of joke?"

"Do I look like I'm laughing?"

No, she thought with dismay. He looked torn; he looked as though he'd rather be anywhere but here. And most of all, he appeared to be genuine.

"What makes you think she's your mother?"

Clearly uncomfortable with her question, he scooted to the edge of the cushion. "It's too long a story to take up your time. I'd better be going. I'll—come back later. When you— well, when you think it'll be okay for me to talk to her."

For a moment, Ileana forgot that she was a doctor and this man was a complete stranger. Frankie and her family had been friends with the Sanderses for many years. In fact, Ileana's mother, Chloe, was worried sick praying that her dear friend would pull through. If this man had something to do with Frankie, Ileana wanted to know about it. She *needed* to know about it, in order to keep her patient safe and cocooned from any stress.

Grabbing his arm, she prevented him from rising to his feet. "I've finished my rounds, Mr. McCleod. I have time for a story."

He glanced toward the plate glass windows surrounding the quiet waiting area. "There's not a whole lot of daylight left. I'm sure it's time for you to go home."

"I can find my way in the dark," she assured him.

Her response must have surprised him, because he looked at her with arched brows.

"All right," he said bluntly. "I'll try to make it short. When I was ten and my brother eight, Frankie McCleod, our mother, left the family." Reaching to his pocket, he pulled out a leather wallet and extracted a photo. As he handed the small square to Ileana, he said, "That was twenty-nine years ago, and we never heard from her again. At least us boys never heard from her. We can't be certain about our father. He never spoke of her. But a few days ago, we found out that Frankie Cantrell had been corresponding through the years with an old friend of hers in the town where we lived. She has to be Frankie McCleod Cantrell."

Dropping her hand away from his arm, Ileana took the photo from him and closely examined the grainy black and white image. Two young boys, almost the same height and both with dark hair, stood next to a young woman wearing an A-line dress and chunky sandals. Her long hair was also dark and parted down the middle. If this was Frankie Cantrell, she'd changed dramatically. But then, nearly thirty years could do that to a person.

"Oh, dear, this is—well, my family and I have been friends with the Cantrells for years. We never heard she had another family. At least, I didn't. I can't say the same for Mother, though." She handed the photo back to him, while wondering if it was something he always carried with him. "The woman in the picture—she's very beautiful. I can't be sure that it's Frankie. I was only a small child when she first came here. I don't recall how she looked at that time."

He lifted his hat from his head and pushed a hand through his hair. It was thick, the color of a dark coffee bean and waved loosely against his head. The shine of it spoke of good health, but Ileana wasn't looking at him as a doctor. No, for the first time in years she was looking at a man as a woman, and the realization shook her even more than his strange story.

He released a heavy breath, then said, "I wasn't expecting to run into this sort of roadblock—I mean, with Frankie being ill. I'm sure you're thinking I should have called first. But this…well, it's not something you can just blurt out over the phone. Besides, if I'd alerted her I was coming, she might have been…conveniently away."

Ileana didn't bother to hide her frown. "Not for a minute. Frankie isn't that sort of woman."

He looked at her. "Do you know what kind of woman she was thirty years ago?"

The question wasn't sharp, but there was an intensity to his voice that caused her cheeks to warm. Or was it just the husky note in his drawl that was making her feel all hot and shivery at the same time? Either way, she had to get a grip on herself and figure out how best to handle this man. If that was possible.

"No. But I hardly think a person's moral values could change that much."

Mac McCleod rose to his feet. "A person can change overnight, Doctor. You know that as well as I."

Not the human heart, she wanted to tell him. But singing Frankie's praises to this man wouldn't help matters at the moment. She wasn't sure what would help this cowboy or how to provide it—other than to let him see Frankie, which at this point was out of the question. If this man was Frankie's son, the shock of seeing him might send her patient into cardiac arrest.

Rising to her feet, she said, "What are your plans? Do you have a place to stay?"

As soon as the questions slipped past her lips, she realized they were probably too personal. Yet she was moved by his plight.

"I have a room rented at a hotel here in town." His dark gaze landed smack on her face. "The rest depends on you."

The man would be leaving the hospital in a few minutes. Her heartbeat should have been returning to its normal pace; instead it was laboring as though she was climbing nearby Sierra Blanca.

"I'm not sure I understand, Mr. McCleod."

A grin suddenly dimpled his cheeks, and she felt like an idiot as her breath caught in her throat.

"I have a feeling we're going to get to know one another very well, Doc. You might as well start calling me Mac."

Ileana cleared her throat. "All right—Mac. Why do your plans depend on me?"

He folded his arms against his chest as his gaze lazily inspected her. For the first time in years, Ileana was horribly aware of her bare face, the homeliness of her plain appearance.

"I can't leave town until I see Ms. Cantrell, and right now it looks as though you're calling the shots as to when that might be," he said.

Ileana not only felt like an idiot but she

needed to add imbecile to the self-description. Normally, her mind was sharp, but this man seemed to be turning her brain to useless gray pudding.

"Oh—uh—yes." Hating herself for getting so flustered, she threw her attention into digging a prescription pad and pen from her lab coat pocket. "Do you have a phone number you can give me? Just in case Ms. Cantrell's condition changes."

He gave his cell phone number to her, then asked, "Are you expecting her to improve in the next day or two—at least, enough for visitors?"

As Ileana folded the piece of paper with the phone number, she carefully chose her words. "Honestly, no. And that's if no complications pop up."

"You do expect her to survive, don't you?"

There was a real look of concern on his face, and Ileana tried to imagine what he must be going through at this moment. He'd traveled hundreds of miles to search for a woman who might be his mother, only to find her desperately ill.

She reached across the small space separating them and folded her hand around his. "I'm doing all I can to make sure she does."

Was it surprise or confusion she saw flickering in his brown eyes before he glanced away? Either way she could see he wasn't nearly as cool as he wanted her to believe. The idea drew her to him just that much more. She knew what it was like to try to hide her emotions, to not allow people to see that she was hurting or troubled.

"Thank you for giving me your time," he murmured. "I'll be checking back with you."

Dropping her hand, she stepped back. "You're very welcome."

"Goodbye, Ms. Sanders."

He cast her one last look, then turned and strode quickly toward an exit that would take him to the parking lot.

As Ileana watched him walk away, she wondered why he'd called her Ms. Sanders. Everyone, even those who had known her for years, didn't think of her as a woman. She was Doc or Doctor. A physician and nothing more.

"Who was *that?*"

At the sound of Renae's voice, Ileana turned her head to see the nurse had walked

Chapter Two

"Ripp, I must have been crazy when I told you to stay home and let me come out here," Mac said into the cell phone. "Nothing is going right."

Two hours had passed since Mac left the hospital, and during that time, he'd continually tried to call his brother back in Texas. But Ripp, and the majority of the sheriff's department, had been on a manhunt most of the evening for a hit-and-run driver. Subsequently, Ripp had just now found time to return his call.

"What do you mean?" Ripp asked. "Did you find the ranch okay?"

"I did," Mac answered as he sat on the side of the hotel bed, his elbows resting on his knees. "A maid was the only person I talked to. She informed me that Ms. Cantrell was in the hospital in Ruidoso."

"Hospital?"

The shock in Ripp's voice mirrored Mac's feelings. That Frankie might be in ill health or dead was something that neither brother had really wanted to consider. After all, if this Frankie were really their mother, she would only be about sixty years old. But a relatively young age didn't always equal good health.

"Yeah. I drove back to Ruidoso and went to the hospital thinking I could talk to her there. No such luck. Her doctor says she's too ill to see me."

"What's wrong with her?"

"The doctor wouldn't tell me much. I was so damned aggravated at the moment that I can't remember everything she said regarding Frankie's health."

"She?"

"Frankie's doctor. It's a woman. And from what she told me, her family and the Cantrells have been friends for years. She—uh—told me that Frankie has a son and daughter. Quint and Alexa, I think she called them."

"Oh." Several long moments passed as Ripp digested this news, and then he finally asked, "Did this doctor know anything about Frankie's past?"

Ripp's question caused the image of Dr. Sanders to parade to the front of Mac's mind. She'd been as plain as white flour. The type of woman he normally wouldn't glance at twice. Yet her gentleness had touched him in a way that had been totally unexpected.

Clearing his throat, he said, "I asked. She doesn't know anything about it. From what she says, Frankie is a respected woman. That ought to tell you the doctor is in the dark."

Ripp sighed. "We don't really know what Frankie is, Mac. That's why you're there. To find out. So when did this doctor think you might be able to see Frankie?"

"Several days, at least."

"Oh. Well, you might as well come home, Mac. There's no use in you hanging around Ruidoso for that long. Or do you think you ought to see her children?"

"And say what?" Mac asked sarcastically. "Hi, y'all, I'm your half brother?"

Ripp growled back at him. "What the hell is the matter with you, Mac? You're nearly forty years old! It's not like you're that ten-year-old little boy, staring out the window with tears on your cheeks. We're not going to let the woman keep hurting us, are we?"

Mac shoved out a heavy breath. His brother was right. He had to get a grip on his emotions and view this whole thing as a man, not that little boy who'd had his heart ripped out so long ago.

"I tell you, Ripp. The news that she had a son and daughter knocked my boots out from under me. I just never imagined her having other babies. Did you? I mean, if she didn't want us, why the heck would she have had more children? Doesn't make a lick of sense to me."

"We don't know that she didn't want us, Mac. Dad told Rye that she wanted us."

"Hell," Mac muttered. "Rye was probably just trying to make you feel better. You'd been stabbed with a butcher knife at the time, remember? He probably thought you couldn't handle any more pain."

Ripp chuckled under his breath. "I can handle anything you can take and more, big brother."

In spite of his frustration, a smile tugged at Mac's lips. If anyone could make him forget his troubles, it was his brother. And even though they were sometimes as different as night and day, there was a bond between them tougher than barbed wire.

"Yeah, you probably can," he told him as he glanced at the digital clock on the night-stand. He was getting hungry. Besides that, the small hotel room was beginning to close in on him. "Look, Ripp, I'm gonna go out and find something to eat. It's been a hell of a day, and I'm beat. I'll call you tomorrow—after I find out more."

"So you're not coming home?"

"No way. I've started on this journey and I don't mean to cut it short. I'm going to camp in the hospital until Dr. Sanders gets her belly full of me. She'll have to give in sooner or later."

"Poor woman. She's not going to know what hit her," Ripp murmured more to himself than to Mac. "Just try to be your charming self, Mac. We don't want anyone out there thinking we're a pair of arrogant Texans."

Mac chuckled. "Why not—we are, aren't we?"

"Go eat. I've got to go help Lucita. Elizabeth is having a squalling fit about something. I'll call you tomorrow."

His brother cut the call, and Mac closed the

instrument in his hand. Ripp had a beautiful wife, a twelve-year-old son and a baby daughter. His family adored him. He had something to live for, something to come home to at night. He was blessed. And Mac was happy for him.

Yet there were times that Mac looked at his brother and wondered what it would feel like to have those same things. Oh, yeah, he'd had a wife once. But Brenna hadn't been a wife in the real sense of the word. She'd been more like a permanent date. Someone to go out with for a night of fun. Someone to have sex with. Giving him children had not been in her plans. And giving him love, the sort that came from deep within a person, was something she'd been incapable of. But then, Mac couldn't put all the blame on Brenna for their failed marriage. At first he'd gotten exactly what he'd wanted—a party girl. And for a while he'd been perfectly content with their life together. Then as time went by, the partying had begun to wear thin, and his life and marriage started to look more and more shallow. He'd begun to yearn for something more lasting and meaningful. Like raising kids in a real home. Brenna hadn't married him under those terms, and when he'd asked her to change, she'd laughed all the way to the office of a divorce lawyer.

Now, after that humiliating lesson, he felt like a fool for ever thinking a good timin' guy like him had once dreamed he could be a father to a house full of kids. Now he told himself it was better to simply enjoy women on brief, but frequent, occasions and forget about ever having a family.

Several miles east of Ruidoso, smack in the middle of the Hondo Valley, Ileana shifted down her pickup truck as it rattled across the low wooden bridge that crossed the Hondo River. The truck was old, and the speedometer had rolled over so many times that she'd lost count. For the past two years her father, Wyatt, had pestered her to buy a new one. After all, she had heaps of money and not a lot to do with it.

But Ileana didn't want a new truck. What would be the use of shaking it over a dirt road every day? she'd argued. Besides, why did she need a new vehicle when the only place she ever went was to work and back home? She was a practical person, and when something worked as it should, she didn't see any point in changing it.

Across the river, the dirt road made a gradual climb into open meadows dotted with ponderosa and piñon pine. On either side of the road, cattle and horses stood at hay mangers, chomping alfalfa in the falling twilight of a late February day.

The Bar M Ranch had been Ileana's home for all her life and her mother's before that. Her grandfather, Tomas Murdock, had built the place from the ground up and turned it into one of the most profitable ranches in southern New Mexico.

But the Bar M hadn't been her grandfather's only interest. He'd been a gambler and a bit of a womanizer, the result of which had produced illegitimate twins. The babies had been left on the doorstep of the Bar M Ranch house, and for weeks no one had known who'd parented them. It had been a shocking event that had rocked all of Lincoln County.

So Ileana wasn't a stranger to odd stories, and the one that Mac McCleod had told her this evening—well, it sounded like more than an odd circumstance to her. Could he possibly be a son from Frankie's past life? And if he hung around like he'd promised, how would the woman react to seeing him again?

The questions had been stewing in Ileana's

head ever since Mac had left the hospital, and now she decided she couldn't go home to her little place on the mountain until she stopped by the main ranch house and had a talk with her mother. If anyone might know about Frankie's past, it would be Chloe.

Five minutes later, she parked the truck behind the pink stucco hacienda and entered a gate that opened to a center courtyard. In the summer months, her parents were always having barbecues and other parties. Her brother, Adam, and his wife, Maureen, often brought their family to join in the fun. So did her sister, Anna, and her husband, Miguel. Even Ileana's aunts, Justine and Rose, made frequent trips to the Bar M with their grandchildren. The crowd of family and friends made the oval swimming pool and courtyard a lively place. But this evening, a cold wind was whipping through the bare garden and ruffling the plastic cover over the pool. The lawn chairs were stacked beneath the covered ground-level porch that followed the square shape of the house.

When Ileana stepped inside the kitchen, she found Cesar, her mother's longtime cook, laying out plates and silverware on a round pine table.

The old cowboy looked up and smiled as he spotted Ileana. "Good evenin', Doc. You stayin' for supper?"

Ileana walked over to the tall, wiry man and kissed his leathery cheek. From the time Cesar had been fifteen years old, he'd worked on the Bar M. After forty years of dealing with fractious horses and several broken bones to show for it, Chloe had relegated him to the kitchen. Now after twenty years of stirring up ranch grub, he could safely be called a hell of a good cook.

"I hadn't planned on it, Cesar, but if you have plenty, I will. Where's Mother? Is she in from the barn yet?"

"She came in a few minutes ago. You might find her in the den."

"Thanks," Ileana told him, then quickly left the kitchen.

The den was quiet and so was the living room. Ileana eventually found Chloe in her bedroom changing into clean clothes.

"Hi, honey!" Chloe said with a bright smile. "You must have stopped by 'cause you knew I'd be lonely tonight."

Ileana sat down on a cedar chest positioned at the foot of a large, varnished pine bed. "Lonely? Isn't Dad here?"

The petite woman finished the last button on her blouse and reached up to whip the towel off her wet hair. Chloe had been a horse lover since she was old enough to sit in the saddle, and she'd made a life breeding and training racing stock. The job was physically strenuous, and now that Chloe was sixty-two, Ileana was beginning to wonder how long she could keep up with the demands of the business. But though she might be small in stature, Chloe was an iron lady. Ileana figured, God willing, her mother would still be working up into her eighties.

"Sanders Gas Exploration has just purchased a competing company, and your father has gone to Oklahoma to tie up all the loose paperwork."

Ileana was incredulous. At a time when her father should have been slowing down, he seemed to be going hell-bent for leather. "He's expanding? Again? Mom, when are you two going to retire and travel the world?"

Chloe laughed as she briskly rubbed her short auburn hair. "Honey, don't ever look for your parents to go galloping around the world for any length of time. Maybe a short vacation now and then. We have too much we want to do."

"But it's work," Ileana complained.

Chloe settled a pointed look at her daughter. "And isn't that what your life is all about?"

Ileana certainly couldn't argue that point. Most every waking hour she spent at her private medical clinic or at the hospital. Even if she wasn't a workaholic, traveling and socializing wasn't her style.

"Okay. So I can't make that argument. But as a doctor I can tell you to slow down."

Chloe laughed. "And as your mother, I can tell you to quit being so fussy." She hung the damp towel on a door hook and began to run a comb through her hair. "So are you going to have dinner with me tonight? Cesar has made goulash and corn bread. He knows I love goulash and your father hates it, so he makes it for me whenever Wyatt is gone."

Chloe started toward the door, and Ileana slowly rose to her feet to follow her out of the bedroom. "I suppose I can stay long enough to eat, but then I've got to get home and go over several test results. I…actually, I stopped by to talk to you about something."

"Oh?" Chloe tossed her a look of concern as the two of them walked along a hallway. "Has something happened? Are you feeling okay?"

"I'm tired. That's the only thing wrong with me, and I'll tell you all about it when we get to the kitchen."

"You've intrigued me now," Chloe said with a smile. Then with a happy groan, she reached over and curled her arm tightly around her daughter's shoulders. "I love you, sweetie. I'm glad you stopped by. No matter what the reason."

Her mother's display of affection was as commonplace as breathing, but Ileana never took it for granted. She'd seen too much suffering in her life to know that there were plenty of unloved people in this world. They marched through her office complaining of one malady after another when their real problem was loneliness.

The idea had her wondering about Mac McCleod's life and what he must have gone through if the story he'd told about his mother was true. It was hard for Ileana to imagine growing up without her mother's love, her constant hugs and kisses. Had the tough cowboy with the sexy brown eyes missed out on being cuddled and praised, or had a stepmother given him and his brother those things? she wondered.

That part of Mac McCleod is none of your

business, Ileana. Just stick to the facts and concentrate on keeping your patient away from any undue stress.

The little voice of warning continued to pester her until the two women entered the kitchen and seated themselves at the small dining table.

"Okay, honey, what's this thing you wanted to discuss with me?" Chloe asked as she spooned a hefty amount of goulash onto her plate. "I hope you haven't stopped by to tell me that Frankie's condition has gotten worse."

"No. Actually, I think she's slightly improved from yesterday, but her lungs still have a long way to go before I can pronounce them clear."

"Damn woman," Chloe muttered. "She should have had heart surgery a year ago when you advised her to."

Ileana sighed. Frankie wasn't the first stubborn patient she'd encountered. Over the eleven years she'd been a practicing physician, Ileana had run into her fair share, and when a patient refused treatment it always left her feeling frustrated and helpless. "That's true. Her lungs are going to keep giving her problems if she doesn't get her heart sound. But she's afraid."

Chloe frowned. "Well, aren't we all afraid of medical procedures? But if we're smart, we do them, because we want to be well and at our best. Life is too short to simply exist. I want to live my God-given days to the fullest."

Ileana thoughtfully stirred sugar into her iced tea. "Yes, but you have lots to live for. I'm not sure that Frankie views life the same as you, Mother. Losing Lewis has devastated her. Just like it would devastate you if Daddy died."

"Of course losing Wyatt would crush me! He's the love of my life. But I'd have to go on doing the very best that I could. To do any less would be dishonorable to Wyatt and you children."

Yes, her mother would see it that way, Ileana thought. But Chloe was a scrapper. As very young women, she and her two sisters had struggled and sacrificed to keep the Bar M going when others would have given up. Frankie didn't have that same fighting spirit. Could her past life be some of the reason for her lack of grit? Ileana wondered.

"Mother, speaking of children, have you ever heard Frankie mention that she had other children?"

Across the table, Chloe's fork stopped midway to her mouth. "Other children? What kind of question is that?"

"It's not some sort of joke, if that's what you're thinking. Besides, you know I don't joke."

Chloe rolled her eyes. "Unfortunately, I do know. But let's not get into that now. What are you getting at? The idea of Frankie having other children is preposterous."

Ileana reached for a piece of cornbread. "You wouldn't be saying that if you'd met Mac McCleod."

Her expression puzzled, Chloe repeated the name. "I've never heard the name. Who is he? Where did you meet him?"

"He's a deputy sheriff from Bee County, Texas. He showed up at the hospital wanting to see Frankie."

Her expression full of concern now, Chloe leaned forward. "You didn't allow him to see her, did you?"

Her mother's sudden anxiousness was suspicious. "You know I'm not allowing anyone in to see her except Quint, Alexa and Abe."

Chloe glanced down at her plate but didn't attempt to resume eating. Ileana could tell that her thoughts were whirling.

"Was it official business?" her mother asked.

"No. Personal." Ileana stabbed a piece of macaroni with her fork. She didn't like giving people she loved bad news. And she had a deep feeling that Mac McCleod's appearance was going to shake up more than a few around here. Especially Alexa and Quint. What would they think about having two half brothers? "He—uh—he says he thinks Frankie might be his long-lost mother. In fact, he seems almost certain of it."

"My God, Ivy! You can't be serious!"

She couldn't remember the last time her mother had called her Ivy, the nickname her father had given her shortly after she'd been born. He'd considered Ileana too long and formal for a tiny baby girl. But by the time she'd reached high school age, Ileana had outgrown the nickname. Now, the only people who sometimes called her Ivy were her father and her brother, Adam. Apparently, her mother was completely distressed tonight.

"Yes, Mother. It seemed incredulous to me, too. But the man isn't a flake. Far from it. He seemed more than legitimate and very determined. He showed me an old snapshot of him and his brother and his mother before she'd left the family. If you took off thirty years, the woman did resemble Frankie."

"An old photograph doesn't prove anything. What was this man like? Did he look like he could be related to Frankie?" she asked, then shook her head with disgust. "What the hell am I doing asking that question? There's just no way. No way at all that Frankie had other children. She would have told me."

Just conjuring the image of Mac in her brain was enough to leave Ileana's mouth dry, and she quickly reached for her tea. "He's a tall, very handsome guy. A cowboy type. A typical Texan," she added, even though there had been nothing typical at all about the man, she thought.

Ileana took several sips of tea while her mother sat in silence. Chloe was either stunned or scared, and Ileana couldn't figure which.

"What's wrong, Mother? You do know something, don't you?"

"You can't let this man see Frankie," she suddenly blurted. "At least, not until we find out more about him."

"Well, I'd already planned on that. Why?" With a heavy sigh, Chloe went back to eating but not with the same gusto as when they'd first sat down at the table.

"Look, Ileana, when I first met Frankie, almost thirty years ago, she was just traveling through the area. She'd left Texas and a husband behind. He was making some frightening threats against her, and at that time she was in the process of getting a divorce and was going by the name of Robertson. She said she'd reverted back to her maiden name."

Ileana's thoughts were spinning. She'd not even known that Frankie had been married before. Apparently that was a part of her life she didn't want others knowing about, and if that was true, she probably wanted to keep other things secret. Like two more sons? The whole idea was shocking.

"When you first met her, did she ever mention what her married name was while she'd lived in Texas?" Ileana asked.

Chloe shook her head. "No. She didn't tell me. And I wasn't about to ask. I only knew that she needed a friend. I could tell that she was a bit traumatized, but what woman wouldn't be? The man had threatened to kill her. And he was a farmer, a respected member of the community, or so she'd said. She'd run because she'd figured if she'd tried to get help, no one would have believed her complaints."

Ileana thoughtfully pushed the goulash around her plate. "Mac didn't mention anything about farming. He said his father had been a sheriff. Maybe Frankie isn't the woman he's looking for. But most of the things he said adds up, Mother."

"How old was this—Mac—as you call him?"

Color instantly bloomed on Ileana's face. Now why had she come out with his first name, as though she knew the man on a personal basis? "My age, I think. He told me his mother left the family when he was ten and his brother eight. And that she's been gone twenty-nine years."

"Oh, dear."

Looking across the table, Ileana spotted tears in her mother's eyes.

"No matter how hard I try, Ileana, I can't imagine Frankie doing such a thing. She loves her children more than her own life. In fact, I've always told her that she smothered them too much. While they were growing up, she was frightened to turn her back for one instant in fear that something would happen to them."

"Well, it's hard to speculate what might have taken place in Texas. Could be that Frankie didn't have much choice," Ileana said thoughtfully. "If the man was threatening her, she might have been forced to leave her boys."

Chloe shook her head emphatically. "But she would have gone back for them. Somehow, someway, she would have gone back."

"Obviously she didn't," Ileana countered. "In fact, she's never mentioned them to you. Doesn't that seem odd?"

"Odd? Hell, no. It seems downright mean," Chloe shot back, then with a weary sigh, she reached across the table and covered Ileana's hand with hers. "Honey, when will you be seeing this man again?"

Ever since he'd disappeared through the hospital door, Ileana had been asking herself that same question. A huge part of her was thrilled at the idea of seeing him again, but the practical side cowered at the very thought. Mac McCleod was hardly the sort of man she would ever dream of consorting with. As if a man with his striking looks would ever think of giving her the time of day, she thought wryly. Everything about the man said he liked fast, showy horses and his women just the same. And Ileana was as far from that category as one could get.

"Tomorrow. Or so he said. I do have his telephone number."

Chloe heaved out a breath of relief. "Good. I want you to give him a call and invite him to the ranch tomorrow night. For dinner."

"Mom! Have you gone daft? I'm not going to do such a thing! I've just now met the man!"

"Look, Ivy, this is crucial!" Chloe pleaded. "You don't want anything happening to Frankie, do you?"

What about your daughter? Ileana wanted to ask. Being around Mac McCleod was difficult on her heart. She wasn't sure it could withstand the strain of being in his company for a whole evening.

"Of course I don't want anything happening to Frankie. She's my patient and a friend."

"All right then." Chloe gave Ileana's hand one last pat and then leaned back in her chair. "I need to talk to this man and find out what's really going on."

"If you have a notion that you can change his mind about seeing Frankie, forget it. I doubt the man has ever uttered the word *sur-*

render. Unless he was yelling it at a fleeing criminal."

Seeming not to hear Ileana's warning, Chloe continued. "Quint and Alexa don't know anything about this yet, do they?"

"No. But I suggested that he talk to them."

"Oh, God, what is this going to do them?" Chloe mumbled worriedly. "They believe their mother is a saint."

Across from her Ileana picked up her fork and tried to muster up the hunger she'd felt earlier this afternoon. The day had been long and exhausting, and she'd hardly had time to eat three bites of a dry turkey sandwich. But now all she wanted to do was go home and get this telephone call to Mac over with.

Back in Ruidoso, Mac had just returned to his motel room after a meal in a nearby restaurant. As he stretched out on the bed and reached for the remote control, the ring of his cell phone caught him by surprise. He'd not expected Ripp to call again tonight.

Pulling the phone from his jeans pocket, he was surprised to spot a local number illuminated. No one here had this number, except Dr. Sanders!

"Hello. Mac McCleod here."

"Uh... Mac—this is... Dr. Sanders calling."

His heart began to hammer with anticipation, or did a part of the adrenaline spurting through his veins have something to do with hearing her voice? After all, it was a sweet, husky sound. The kind that would sound perfect whispering in his ear.

Damn, Mac, leaving Texas soil has done something to your brain.

Snapping himself to sudden attention, he said, "Yes, Dr. Sanders. Has something happened?"

"If you mean Ms. Cantrell's condition, no. I just spoke with her nurse. She's resting comfortably. I'm calling for an entirely different reason."

There was hesitancy about her words that put Mac on guard. Without thinking, he sat up on the side of the bed and stared expectantly at the floor. "You've changed your mind about allowing me to see her?"

"Uh—no. I'm...well, I'm calling to ask you to dinner tomorrow night," she said, then rushed on before he could make any sort of response. "I live on a ranch in the Hondo Valley—my parents' ranch—the Bar M. My mother thought you might like to visit with her. Since she's known Frankie for nearly thirty years, she might be able to fill in some pieces of information for you."

Mac hesitated for several seconds before he finally asked, "And why would she want to do that? I got the impression that you and your family want to shelter Frankie at all costs."

He could hear her long sigh, and he was suddenly wondering how she might look with all that dark hair spilling around her pale face, with a sultry little smile on her lips and a sensual glint in her blue eyes. Was it possible he could ever see her like that?

"I do—we do. But we want to consider your side of this thing, too. Besides, Cesar is an excellent cook. If nothing else, you'll get a nice meal."

"And what about the company? Will you be there, too?"

There was a long pause, and Mac could very nearly imagine the blush that was creeping across her face. She reminded him of the timid, high school librarian who'd pursued him a few months ago. Once he'd gotten her in the dark, she'd been shy but sweet and eager. If he played his cards right, he might get lucky and discover that behind her lab coat and sturdy shoes, Dr. Ileana Sanders was just as sweet.

"Yes. I'll be there," she said.

"Great. What time and how do I get there?"

"Meet me at the hospital tomorrow evening at six," she told him. "You can follow me out to the ranch from there."

"Count on me being there," he told her.

"Fine. Good night, Mac."

"Good night, Ms. Sanders."

She cleared her throat. "Please call me Ileana."

A lazy smile spread across his face. "You can count on that, too—Ileana."

She blurted another hasty good-night to him, then ended the call. Mac leaned back on the bed and stared thoughtfully up at the ceiling. Maybe hanging around here in New Mexico for a few more days wasn't going to be as cold and lonely as he first feared.

Chapter Three

The next evening, a few minutes before six, Ileana managed to wind up the last of her hospital rounds and hurriedly changed from her work clothes into a royal-blue sweater dress and a pair of tall, black suede boots. The dress had only been worn once, two years ago, when she'd attended a charity dinner with her parents. Ileana rarely bothered to vary her wardrobe from slacks or professional skirts and mundane blouses. No one bothered to look at her sideways. And if they did, it was because she was a doctor and they wanted to hear what she had to say about a patient or ailment.

But this morning, she'd grabbed the dress from her closet and convinced herself that her mother would be pleased if she dressed for their dinner guest tonight.

Shutting the door on her private workspace, Ileana hurried down the hallway toward the nearest hospital exit. She was almost past the nurses' station, when Renae called out to her.

"Dr. Sanders, is that you?"

Stifling a sigh, Ileana paused and looked back at the nurse. "Yes, it's me, Renae. I'm on my way home. Was there something you needed before I leave?"

The tall nurse with wheat-blond hair and bright blue eyes stepped out from behind the high counter. "No. Everything is quiet." Her gaze ran pointedly over Ileana's dress and boots. "My, oh my, you look—so different! I've never seen you dressed this way! And you're wearing lipstick!"

A faint blush warmed Ileana's cheeks, making them match the shell-pink color she'd swiped over her lips. She felt incredibly self-conscious. Which was absurd. She was thirty-eight years old. She could wear what she wanted, whenever she wanted, she tried to reassure herself. "I break out of my rut once in a while, Renae."

The other woman smiled. "Well, you should do it more often, Doc." Renae's expression turned impish. "You wouldn't want to tell me what the occasion is, would you?"

Renae would be the first one to admit that she did her share of contributing to the hospital gossip grapevine. But Ileana certainly didn't have anything to hide. Her personal life was as flat and uninteresting as a cold pancake.

"Mother is having a dinner guest, and she doesn't like for me to show up in wrinkled work clothes."

Renae started to reply but paused as the sound of approaching footsteps caught both women's attention. Ileana looked around to see Mac McCleod striding directly toward them. He was wearing a jean jacket with a heavy sheepskin collar, and his cowboy hat was pulled low over his forehead; but the moment he neared the two women, he tilted it back and smiled broadly.

"Good evenin', ladies."

Renae gave him one of her sexy smiles, and Ileana thought how perfect a companion the young nurse would be for the Texas cowboy. She was full of life and nothing—not even a man like Mac McCleod—intimidated her. Whereas Ileana felt like Little Red Riding Hood standing next to the big scary wolf.

"Good evening, Mr. McCleod," Renae greeted him. "Fancy seeing you here again."

He glanced briefly at the nurse before settling his eyes on Ileana. The direct gaze heated her body more than a huge shot of whiskey ever could.

"Yes," he said to the nurse. "Dr. Sanders was kind enough to invite me to dinner."

The sound of his voice was low and sultry. Or at least it seemed that way to Ileana. But she could be overreacting. Either way, she was ready to leave the hospital and break the odd tension that had suddenly come over her.

"Oh, how nice," Renae responded while casting a shocked glance at Ileana.

"We'd better be going, Mac. Or we'll be late." Ileana quickly grabbed him by the arm and urged him toward the exit. To Renae, she tossed over her shoulder, "See you tomorrow."

As the two of them headed down the wide corridor, he asked, "What's the rush? Afraid I'm going to pester you to see Frankie before we leave the hospital?"

"No," Ileana replied. "It wouldn't make any

difference how much you pestered me. The answer would still be no. At least for today."

"So she's still too ill for visitors?"

Now that they were away from Renae and nearing a revolving door that would take them outside the hospital, Ileana dropped her hand from his arm and purposely put space between their bodies. Even so, she was intensely aware of his spicy scent, the sensual swagger of his posture and the pleasant drawl to his voice.

"I'm afraid so."

"Are you sure she's getting everything she needs at this hospital? Maybe if you sent her to Albuquerque or Santa Fe? I mean, I'm not doubting your ability as a doctor, but she might need to be in a more high-tech facility."

Ileana paused to pull on the black coat that was draped over her arm, but before she could swing it around her shoulders, he took the garment from her and graciously helped her into it. Ileana couldn't remember the last time a man, other than a relative, had done such a personal thing for her. It made her feel awkward, yet sweetly cared for at the same time.

She'd never been really hurt or abused by any man, but her natural shyness and private nature had kept them at bay for years. Now it was a habit she couldn't seem to break out of. Everyone thought of her as a plain old maid, and she couldn't seem to change her own opinion of herself. But seeing her in this stranger's eyes was giving her new hope.

Looking up at him, she smiled. "I'm sure you mean well, Mac. But there is no high-tech machine that can cure Frankie right now. And even if there were, our hospital here has up-to-date equipment. No, the only thing that can help Frankie is medication and total rest."

He let out a long breath, and she could clearly see that he was frustrated, but his demeanor changed as quickly as the snap of two fingers. Once again he was smiling down at her. For a moment Ileana forgot that they were standing to one side of the door and that people were coming and going behind them. She was momentarily mesmerized by the subtle glint in his brown eyes, the faint dimples bracketing his lips, the dent in his chin.

"Well," he said softly, "that just means I'll have to stay here in Ruidoso longer and get to know you a bit better."

Dropping her head, she cleared her throat as she tried to gather herself together. "Um… we'd better go. It's a fairly long drive to the Bar M," she told him.

Out in the parking lot, a north wind was whipping across the asphalt, rattling the bare limbs of the aspens and shaking the branches of the blue spruce trees. Ileana huddled, shivering inside her coat, as she gave him general directions to the ranch, then climbed into her truck and waited for him to do the same.

Soon a dark, fairly new-looking pickup truck pulled directly behind hers. She steered her own vehicle onto the street while carefully watching in the rearview mirror to make sure he was following. After a maze of turns and several traffic lights, they hit the main highway that would take them east to the Hondo Valley.

The Bar M was nearly thirty miles away and in the daylight, a beautiful drive through the mountains. But night had fallen more than an hour ago. As she drove, Ileana's gaze switched from the white line on the highway to the headlights following a respectable distance behind her, while her thoughts raced faster than the speedometer on the dash panel.

What was the man really trying to do? There was no reason for him to flirt with her. In fact, the whole idea seemed ridiculous. But he had flirted, she mentally argued with herself. At least, it had felt that way to her. So why? Was he still thinking he could charm her into letting him see Frankie?

Yes. That had to be the reason. A man like him didn't look twice at a woman like her for romantic reasons. And during the evening ahead, she was going to do her best to remember that.

Since Mac McCleod was a guest who had never visited the ranch before, Ileana purposely parked in front of the house so that they could enter properly through the main entrance.

When he joined her on the small stone walk leading up to the long porch, he paused to look around at the area lit by a nearby yard lamp.

"This is quite a beautiful place. I'd like to see the ranch and the drive up here in the daylight sometime."

"Yes. Even though it is my home, I never take the scenery for granted," she replied, then gestured toward the house. "Shall we go in? It's very cold this evening."

"It's damn—sorry—it's darn cold to me," he said as he followed her to the door. "It gets cool where I come from but not anything like this. We're lucky if we see a frost, much less snow."

"Oh, come June and July we'll get some very warm weather," she told him. "But with the high altitude the nights remain cool."

She opened the door and gestured for him to enter, but he shook his head and smiled.

"I'd never go before a lady. You lead the way."

Even though Mac's mother had left the family, he'd obviously been raised with manners, Ileana thought. And a whole lot of charm. Something she needed to ignore. But everything inside her was so aware of the man, so pleased to be in his presence. And the reaction made her feel more foolish than she'd ever felt in her life.

As they moved from the foyer into the long living room, Ileana was relieved to find her mother sitting on the couch. The moment Chloe spotted them, she rose to her feet and quickly joined them.

"Mac, this is my mother, Chloe Sanders. Mother, this is Mac McCleod," Ileana promptly introduced.

"Mr. McCleod, I'm very happy you decided to join us tonight," Chloe told him as she reached to shake his hand.

He took her hand, but rather than shake it, he simply held it in a warm, inviting grip. As a smile dimpled his cheeks, Ileana could see her mother succumbing to the man.

"It's my pleasure, ma'am. Having you two ladies for company sure beats the lonely meal I had last night."

Chloe chuckled softly. "Eating alone isn't much fun. But my husband sometimes travels so I have to do it at times. Are you married, Mr. McCleod?"

Mac gave her a lopsided grin. "No. I'm a single man. And call me Mac, ma'am. Ileana already does."

Chloe's brows inched upward as she glanced over at her daughter. Ileana smiled awkwardly as her mother's gaze swept over her sweater dress and her stacked heel boots.

"Does Cesar have dinner ready yet?" Ileana asked quickly.

"I think it will be a few more minutes," Chloe said, then looped her arm through Mac's. "Come along, Mac, and make yourself comfortable. I was just having a small glass of wine. Would you like to join me?"

"Only if Ileana will share one with us," he said.

"Usually Ileana doesn't drink anything but water," Chloe said. "But maybe she'll make an exception tonight—for you," Chloe added.

Ileana didn't know why her mother was speaking in such a coy manner or why Chloe expected her to drink a glass of wine when she knew her daughter didn't like alcohol. But then, this whole issue with Mac McCleod was strange. His presence must be rubbing off on her mother, too, she thought.

"Only a very small glass," Ileana told her.

Mac took a seat in a stuffed armchair situated a few feet from the fireplace, which at the moment was cracking and hissing with a roaring fire. Ileana took a chair across from him and crossed her legs. Then realizing she didn't feel comfortable, she rested both feet flat on the floor and folded her hands in her lap.

Across the room, at a small wet bar, Chloe asked, "So have you been in Ruidoso for long, Mac?"

"Only since yesterday, ma'am."

"How do you like this area?" she asked, as she handed him a glass of wine.

He thanked her, then said, "It's very beautiful. But it's not Texas. No offense, ma'am."

Chloe laughed softly. "I know what you mean, Mac. Texas is your home, so nothing could compare."

"Yeah," he agreed. "That pretty much says how it is."

Chloe handed Ileana a glass with a very short amount of red liquid in the bottom, then took a seat on a nearby couch.

Ileana said, "I'm sorry my father couldn't be with us tonight, Mac. He's away on business right now."

"Is he a cattleman?" Mac asked.

"No. Daddy knows about cattle, but he's mainly an oilman," Ileana explained.

"Wyatt owns and runs a natural gas exploration business," Chloe added. "He was doing that when we married—oh so many years ago."

Mac looked back and forth between the two women. These people were well off financially. Even more than he'd initially thought. "This ranch, do you run stock on it?"

"Oh, yes," Chloe answered. "It's been a working ranch for nearly seventy-five years. For the most part, we raise horses, and I train them for the racetrack."

He looked intrigued now, and Ileana wasn't surprised. Her mother lived and worked in mostly a man's world, at an exciting sport. Whereas Ileana worked at a job that was oftentimes depressing and complicated. Men were rarely drawn to her occupation.

"Thoroughbreds or quarter horses?" he asked Chloe.

"Both."

Mac looked over at Ileana and was struck at how lovely she looked with her face bathed in a golden glow from the fire and the tail of her simple ponytail lying against one shoulder. There was a quiet dreaminess about her expression that was both soothing and inviting at the same time, and he found himself wishing he was going to have dinner with her alone.

"What about you, Ileana? Are you familiar with horses?"

"Ileana is an excellent horsewoman," Chloe spoke up before her daughter could answer his question. "But she rarely takes the time to ride."

"Keeping others well is important to me, Mother."

Chloe smiled, but Mac got the sense that there was sadness behind her expression. As though she didn't quite approve of her daughter's lifestyle.

"Yes. And I'm very proud of you, darling. You know that."

The room went quiet after that, and it suddenly dawned on Mac that he'd been so caught up in conversation with Ileana and her mother that Frankie, the reason for this visit, had totally slipped his mind.

"Ileana tells me you're from Texas, Mac. What part?" Chloe asked.

"South Texas, ma'am. About forty miles north of Corpus Christi. I'm a deputy for Sheriff Langley Nichols in Bee County."

She nodded slightly. "I have a brother-in-law and nephew who both served several terms as sheriff here in Lincoln County. We know all about the dedication you men put in your jobs. You're to be commended."

"Thank you, ma'am."

Ileana's mother smiled. "Call me Chloe."

At that moment, an older man, tall, with a thick head of salt and pepper colored hair, appeared in an open doorway of the room. He politely inclined his head toward Mac, then turned his attention to the mistress of the house.

"Supper's ready, Chloe."

"Thank you, Cesar. We'll be right there."

The two women rose to their feet, and Mac followed behind Ileana as they left the living room and entered an adjoining room to their right. The rectangular space was furnished with a long cedar table that seated ten. The top was made of board planks while the legs had been roughly hewed from small cedar post. The matching chairs were worn smooth from years of use. Above the table, a lamp fashioned like a kerosene lantern hung from a low ceiling and cast a dim glow over the dining area. Across the way, heavy drapes were pushed back from a double window. Beyond the blackened panes, Mac could make out the tall branches of a spruce tree whipping in the cold wind.

In the past year, his brother had married a ranching heiress, a daughter of one of the Sandbur Ranch families. Since then, Mac had had the pleasure of visiting the huge ranch, and he could safely say that this house was nothing like the huge, elaborate homes there. This Bar M Ranch house was much smaller in scale and far more rustic in furnishings and appearance. As Mac helped both women into their chairs, he decided the Sanders family was only concerned with two things. Comfort and practicality.

After Mac took a seat directly across from Ileana, the man called Cesar served them a salad that was full of ripe olives and bits of corn chips. The concoction was so tasty Mac forgot that he didn't like salads.

"Ileana tells me that you've come to Ruidoso to see Frankie Cantrell," Chloe said, once all of them were eating.

Mac hadn't expected her to bring up the subject so bluntly, but he was quickly seeing that Chloe wasn't bashful about speaking her mind.

"That's right. I—we—that is, my brother and I didn't have any idea she was ill. If we'd known I would have put off the trip to a later date."

Chloe thoughtfully chewed a bite of food, then said, "So Frankie didn't have any idea you were coming to New Mexico?"

"No. Ripp and I didn't want to write or call. This matter is something that needs to be dealt with in person. Face-to-face."

Silence settled over the table, and Mac could feel Ileana's gaze settle on him. When he looked across the table at her, there was a shy smile on her face. The sweetness of it caught his attention far more than a wicked wink would have, and he wondered if the high altitude of these desert mountains was doing something to him. Right now they were probably more than seven thousand feet above sea level. Maybe he was getting altitude sickness. Something was definitely making him dizzy.

"I've told Mother about your concerns— that you believe Frankie might be your mother. I hope you don't mind me sharing the information."

"Of course I don't mind," he said. "It's hardly something I'm trying to keep a secret. I can't find answers without asking questions. And questions require explanations."

"Well," Chloe began, "I'll be honest, Mac. Your story floored me. I've known Frankie Cantrell for nearly thirty years. I've never heard her mention having other children. I mean, children from her past."

Mac told himself not to let this morsel of information get to him. A good lawman always gathered all the evidence he could find before he took action. Even when he might be the victim.

"Maybe she wanted to forget she had other children," he suggested.

With a long sigh, Chloe put down her fork and faced him directly. Mac studied her closely, and as he did, he found himself comparing the woman to Ileana. The two didn't match in looks or demeanor, so he assumed Ileana must have taken after her father.

"I'm being honest with you now, Mac. The Frankie Cantrell I know just wouldn't forget her children. It's unfathomable. She's been the most loving, caring mother I've known. She's a good and decent woman. If she is your mother, something dire must have happened in her past to make her leave."

Everything inside Mac went still. This woman knew something. Probably more than she was saying. But he honestly didn't want to hear it from her. For years now, all he'd gotten about his mother was secondhand words and phrases. He wanted to hear it directly from Frankie herself. Otherwise, it wouldn't have the same meaning.

"What makes you say that?" he asked quietly. "Do you know about my mother's past? Where she came from?"

Chloe shook her head. "Only that she came from somewhere in Texas. I've never asked. And she's never told me more."

"So you don't know what her name was before she married Lewis Cantrell?"

"She told me it was Robertson, and I never thought it could be anything else."

Mac shook his head. "Well, that wouldn't have been our mother's married name or her maiden name, which was Anderson, but everything else seems to fit. My brother and I have just learned that Frankie Cantrell had been corresponding with a friend's mother through the years. That's a bit too much of a coincidence."

Concern marred Chloe's face, but whether it was for her friend or for Mac, he had no idea. Most likely the former. Friendship was oftentimes thicker than kinship.

"Have you questioned this woman?"

"Unfortunately she passed away a couple months ago. Our friend, her son, was trying to organize her things and ran across the letters. That's how we happened to find out about them."

"Oh. I'm sorry your friend's mother is no longer with us," Chloe said.

"Mac, this might be too personal," Ileana spoke up, "but have you read the letters? Did they give you any clues?"

His mouth twisted. Now that the sweet doctor had put the question to him, the fact that he and Ripp had refused to inspect the letters sounded inane. They should have scoured every line, every word. Instead, they'd both been reluctant to discover what, if anything, Frankie might have said.

Looking down at his salad, he said, "No.

I couldn't bring myself to look at them. Neither could my brother. We wanted to see what Frankie had to say first, before we let things that had been written in the past sway our feelings. But we do know that both of us are mentioned in the letters."

"I can certainly understand you being reluctant to read them," Ileana said softly. "You have no idea what you might find. Things that could be heartbreaking."

"Well, frankly, I'm not as understanding as my daughter," Chloe said firmly. "Reading the letters might have answered everything for you."

He looked directly at the older woman. "You think so? Reading a letter would be the same as talking in person to your mother? I don't think so."

"I can't speak to my mother, Mac. She died when I was twenty-three and so did my father."

If Chloe expected him to apologize she was going to be disappointed. She was the one who was guilty of speaking out of turn. Especially when she didn't know what sort of life he'd had or anything about his family. She couldn't guess the devastation that Frankie's leaving had caused the McCleod home. His

father had never been the same, and as for
Mac and Ripp, well, he supposed they'd never
been the same either.

"We've all lost family," he said politely.

Chloe suddenly smiled. "Sorry if I sounded
harsh, Mac. I didn't intend to. In fact, I think
I'm beginning to like you. I'm just concerned
about my friend. Surely you understand."

"I do. And for what it's worth, I'm not here
to cause Frankie Cantrell any sort of grief.
Or to harm her in any way. My brother and
I aren't interested in any sort of monetary
gain, whether that be from money, property
or anything else. The only thing we're interested in is knowing if our mother is alive—
if this woman could be the same Frankie."

Chloe nodded in a way that said she understood but still found the whole matter worrisome. "And you can't be a hundred percent
certain of that until you finally speak with
her, will you?"

Mac looked across at Ileana. "That's true.
And Ileana has the final say over that."

Even in the dim light, he could see a faint
pink color stain her cheekbones. The blush
brightened her otherwise pale face.

"Frankie needs to improve greatly before
I allow such a meeting." She looked directly

at Mac. "Why don't you show Mother your photo, Mac? She might be able to recognize if the woman is Frankie Cantrell."

He glanced hesitantly toward Chloe. "I'm not sure your mother wants to see the photo."

Chloe put down her fork and held out her hand in an inviting way. "Of course I want to see it. Whatever you might be thinking, Mac, I can't hide from the truth. No more than you can."

Mac forgot about the food in front of him as he fished the photograph from his wallet and handed it over to Chloe. The woman studied it for long agonizing moments before she finally lifted her head.

"When I first met Frankie she had naturally black hair. Was that the color of your mother's hair?" she asked him.

Mac tilted his head to one side as he allowed himself to remember. "I guess you'd call it that. It looked black until she got out in the sun, and then it had a fiery sort of glow to it. I thought she was the prettiest woman who ever walked the earth."

Chloe's smile was gentle. "I expect we all think that of our mothers." She handed the ragged photo back to Mac. "I can't be for certain, but the woman in the photo looks very much like Frankie Cantrell."

Mac and Ripp had already pretty much come to the logical deduction that the two women had to be the same person. Still, it was a jolt to hear this woman actually say it. Even so, he did his best to remain casual as he stuffed the photo back in his wallet.

"Well, I guess that answers one question," he said quietly.

"But there are so many more questions to come," Chloe stated wisely. "And I have to admit, Mac, that I'm just as anxious as you are to hear them."

Mac agreed, while wondering if he and his brother would be better off if he simply packed his things and headed back to Texas. In all likelihood he'd found Frankie McCleod. She was in ill health but alive. She owned a ranch and had other children. What good would it do now to appear in her life, in her children's lives?

I promise, boys, I'll be back for you. No matter what, Mommy loves you, and I'll come back.

That hastily spoken promise had haunted Mac and Ripp for nearly three decades. If anything, they deserved to know why she'd not kept it.

After a few awkward moments of silence passed, Chloe turned the conversation to other things, and before Mac knew it, he was relating some of the more colorful incidents he'd experienced since becoming a lawman. In turn, Chloe and Ileana recounted stories about their relatives who had spent years in the capacity of sheriff.

Eventually, when the meal was over, Cesar served them coffee and dessert in the living room, but after a few short minutes, Chloe excused herself saying she needed to make a few important phone calls.

The woman's exit left Mac and Ileana alone, with nothing but the sound of the crackling fire and the cold north wind whistling through the spruce trees outside the window.

Mac ate the last bite of cake from his dish and placed it and his empty cup on a nearby coffee table. Then he walked over to the fireplace.

With his back to the flames, he looked pointedly at Ileana. "Your mother knows more about Frankie than she's saying."

Ileana rubbed her palms nervously down

her thighs, then rose to her feet and walked over to stand in front of him. She'd only met him yesterday, yet she felt connected to him in an odd sort of way. Maybe it was because he'd shared such personal troubles with her. Or maybe it was because he'd seemed to look at her. Really look at her.

"I probably shouldn't be saying anything. But Mother told me that when she first met Frankie, she was running from an abusive husband. Is that in character with your father?"

The expression on his rugged face didn't change, but she could see surprise flicker in his eyes and then a shutter lowered and blocked any inkling of his feelings.

"No. Once our mother left, Dad refused to speak of her. But while we were still a family, I never saw him lift a hand to her in any way. Neither did Ripp, or he would have told me."

"There are other ways of abusing a person," she dared to say.

His eyes suddenly softened, and as they settled on her face Ileana felt her insides turning as mushy as a hot chocolate bar.

"That's true," he murmured. "And it's true that two young boys wouldn't know what went on with their parents behind closed doors. But my father was a good man. He loved us and raised us without any help from friends or relatives. And the people in the county liked and respected him. In fact, he was never voted out of office. His failing health finally forced him to retire after fifteen years of service to his community. Does that sound like an abusive man?"

Making people feel better was the very thing that Ileana had dedicated her life to. And more often than not, she couldn't stop her emotions from getting involved. But there was something about Mac that made her feel more deeply, made her ache to give his heart ease. What did that mean?

She sighed. "No. And I only told you what Mother said because I know that you need answers. If you can hang on a few more days, Frankie will be well enough to give them to you."

The wry smile on his lips deepened to a seductive grin, and Ileana's breath lodged somewhere in the middle of her chest.

"Hang on?" he repeated softly. "With you for company I won't have any problem at all hanging on in New Mexico for a while."

The suggestive implication of his words shocked her, but she tried her best to keep a cool mask on her face. The last thing she wanted to do was let him know just how inexperienced she was with men like him— any man in general. And she especially didn't want him knowing that her knees were threatening to buckle beneath his charm.

"Mac, I—"

Before she could form any sort of sensible response, he shocked her further by stepping forward, until the small space separating their bodies had disappeared and she could smell his scent, feel the heat radiating from his body.

"From the first moment we met, I've been wondering something about you," he drawled in a low, sultry voice.

She tried not to shiver as his gaze made lazy trails over her face. "What is that?" she asked, unaware that her own voice had dropped to a husky whisper.

"How you would look like this."

With one smooth movement, his hand moved to the back of her head and released the barrette holding her hair. Once he pulled the clasp away, the silky tresses spilled onto her shoulders and tumbled against her cheeks.

She tried to make herself step away, to admonish him for being so forward and impertinent, but all she managed to do was stand paralyzed and breathless as his long fingers pushed into her hair, combed the loose curls against her collarbone.

"You—you've lost your mind."

Her strangled words were said with more awe than accusation, making the grin on his face a slash of satisfaction.

"Not yet. But I will if I don't do this."

Before she could ask what *this* was, his face dipped to hers, and then she could see nothing but a glimpse of hard jaw, flared nostrils and a perfectly chiseled mouth descending toward hers.

The shock that he was going to kiss her short-circuited her senses. Even if she'd wanted to run, she was helpless, caught in his spell like a horse against a tight rein.

Softly, his lips settled over hers and then running was all but forgotten as the wild, forbidden taste of him swirled her to a place she'd never been.

Chapter Four

Mac was totally lost in the taste of Ileana's kiss, the feel of her soft body next to his, when the faint sound of a throat being cleared suddenly jarred his senses.

Like a kid being caught with his finger in the Sunday dinner dessert, he thrust himself away from Ileana and glanced across the room to see Chloe standing in an open doorway, then back to Ileana's shocked face.

Oh, hell, what had he done?

He opened his mouth to try to make some sort of apology to Ileana, but before he could muster a word, she whirled and ran from him, nearly crashing into her mother along the way.

The urge to run after her was about to push Mac's boots off the hearth, when she disappeared into the foyer and then the sound of the front door slamming told him his efforts would be wasted. Ileana was leaving without a word.

"It looks as though I've interrupted something," Chloe said with faint surprise as she glanced at him then to the foyer where her daughter had made a quick exit.

Knowing his face was red, he said sheepishly, "I don't know what to say. Except that I'm sorry. We were talking and—well, I… Your daughter is a lovely woman and I…got a little carried away. Please forgive me. You were both so kind to invite me to dinner this evening. Now I've made a mess of everything."

Walking deeper into the room, Chloe smiled at him as though nothing was wrong. "Nonsense. My daughter is a grown woman. A little kiss isn't going to hurt her. At least, not your brand."

Relief poured through him. Although he wasn't exactly sure why Chloe's opinion of him should matter that much, it did. She was

Ileana's mother, and he didn't want to offend either woman.

"It doesn't look like Ileana feels that way," he said dismally. "I doubt she'll want to speak with me again."

Chloe shook her head. "Ileana never harbors bad feelings toward anyone. If she's angry, she'll forgive you."

Regret fell on his shoulders like a lead weight. Ileana had raced out of the room like the devil himself was on her heels, he thought. If anger hadn't been pushing her, then fright had and to Mac that was equally bad. He was a protector at heart. He didn't want a woman fearing him for any reason.

Wiping a hand over his face, he turned an apologetic smile on his hostess. "Well, I think I've done enough damage for one night. I'd better be going. Thank you for the great dinner. And your hospitality."

Mac started to move past her, but she quickly stepped in his path.

"Not so fast, Mac. I'd like to talk to you before you leave." She gestured toward the couch. "Why don't you have a seat? I don't want you to bolt out on me like my daughter just did," she added wryly.

Trying to hide his surprise, Mac moved

over to the couch and took a seat at one end while Chloe eased down in an armchair opposite him.

"Is this something about Frankie Cantrell?" he asked with a puzzled frown.

Smiling wryly, she said, "I guess you could say so. In a roundabout way. You're here to see my friend, and I feel like the least I can do is offer my home to you while you're waiting for her to get well."

Confusion puckered his brow. "Your home?"

Nodding, Chloe used one hand to gesture about the room. "Yes. This house. The Bar M. I'd like for you to stay with us. And—" she added quickly as he opened his mouth to protest "—please don't dismiss my invitation before hearing me out. You'll be far more comfortable here than you would be in a stifling hotel room."

To say that he was shocked would have been a mild understatement. "I don't doubt that. But I wouldn't want to be an inconvenience to you. Besides that, I'm not sure how my staying here would look to your family and friends."

She chuckled softly. "Mac, my husband will be home tomorrow evening. And even if he weren't, it would hardly matter to him. He welcomes all my friends to the Bar M."

"But you hardly know me," Mac pointed out.

He could feel her gaze sizing him up, and something about her keen scrutiny told him she was a woman who rarely missed a beat about people and situations. So what was she really thinking about him? That he was actually a liar or a con man looking for money from Frankie? Lord, the woman's money or things weren't what he wanted.

"I know you well enough to know that I'd like to help you."

"What about Frankie? She's your friend. If I stay here, it might cause hard feelings between you and her family."

Chloe was quick to reply. "I appreciate your concern, Mac. But Quint and Alexa are open-minded people. You staying on my ranch is hardly going to cause a rift between our families. Frankie has been a good friend for many years. I want to help her, too. And you being here just might do that. And anyway, it looks as though the Cantrells might have to get ready for some new relatives in the family…whether they want them or not."

If Frankie hadn't wanted to see him and

Ripp for twenty-nine years, he could hardly imagine her being thrilled at his appearance in her life. As for her two children, Mac couldn't imagine what they were going to think when they discovered they had two half brothers in Texas. At the moment, it was almost more than his brain could process.

"I'll be honest, Chloe. The idea of staying here on your beautiful ranch sounds a heck of a lot nicer than holing up in a hotel room. But I'm not used to—"

"Accepting people's hospitality?"

Opening one's home to a stranger was far more than hospitality, Mac thought. He couldn't remember anyone ever offering him such a personal invitation. Even his ex in-laws had never invited him and Brenna to spend much time in their home. Their visits with the Phillips had been brief and a bit uncomfortable. But then, Brenna's parents had always believed that Mac had ruined their daughter by turning her into a party girl. He'd never bothered to defend himself against the accusation. There'd been no point in hurting them further by revealing to them that Brenna had never been the innocent wife who stayed home, baked cookies and planned a nursery.

"I guess you could say that."

She smiled at him. "Well, this will be a good time for you to start."

"But what about Ileana? I don't think—"

"Ileana no longer lives here in the main house with us. Her schedule is oftentimes hectic, and she likes her solitude. She lives on up the mountain in her own house."

Mac hadn't expected that. He'd already pictured Ileana as the homebody sort. The type who wouldn't leave her parents unless it was necessary. But then, as a deputy he'd learned that first impressions could be off base. There could be other things about Ileana Saunders that he'd gotten wrong. But her kiss wasn't one of them. He'd be safe in saying it had been the softest, sweetest thing he'd ever tasted.

"Oh. She didn't tell me that."

"Ileana doesn't do much talking about herself."

Maybe no one had ever asked her to, Mac thought. And he suddenly realized he was a bit disappointed in hearing that Ileana lived elsewhere. Having her company around this place would have been nice.

He rubbed his fists down his thighs, then awkwardly rose to his feet. "All right, Chloe. I accept your invitation. And hopefully Frankie will be well soon and you won't have to put up with me for long."

Leaving her chair, Chloe accompanied him to the door. "Trust me, Mac, you won't be a burden."

Pausing at the door, Mac turned and shook Chloe's hand. "Thank you, Chloe. I'll be out with my things tomorrow afternoon."

She patted the top of his hand in a reassuring way. "Come at any time you'd like. If you need me, I'll probably be down at the barn. Otherwise, Cesar will be around, and he'll make sure you have everything you need."

Mac thanked her again and then bade the woman a good-night.

Outside, as he walked to his truck, cold wind whistled through the canyon and shook the nearby fir trees. But this time the cold didn't turn his wishful thoughts to the warm climes of South Texas. Instead, he looked toward the mountain rising up behind the Bar M Ranch house and wondered how soon he'd be able to see Ileana again.

The next afternoon at Murdock Family Clinic in Ruidoso, the private health center Ileana established several years ago, she peered into the ears of an elderly gentleman sitting on the edge of the examining table, then stepped back to give him her diagnosis.

"Mr. Hanover, how long have you been having trouble hearing?"

The frail man with snow-white hair frowned blankly at her. "Huh?"

Ileana deliberately raised her voice several decibels. "Your ears are going to be fine. I'm going to write you a prescription, and I want you to use it every day for the next week. Then I want you to come back here to the office, and I'll wash your ears out."

He pointed an accusing finger at her. "Why can't you wash 'em out today? You gonna make me come back so you can get more money out of me?"

Ileana didn't know whether she wanted to laugh or sigh as she used the next few minutes to explain to her patient that his ears were full of wax and that she couldn't safely remove it until it was softened.

"I won't charge you for next week's visit, Mr. Hanover," she assured him as she helped him out of the examining room. "You just make sure you keep the appointment that Evaline gives you at the front desk."

Out in the hallway, Ada, her longtime assistant, immediately appeared to take Mr. Hanover off Ileana's hands. The registered nurse was close to Ileana's age and divorced. For the past ten years she'd helped Ileana build the clinic up to the busy place it was today.

"Let me take care of this, Doc," she said to Ileana. "You go grab a bite to eat."

"Thanks, Ada. I'll be in my office if you need me." She turned, then paused as another concern crossed her mind. "Oh, Ada, did you give Tommy those sample inhalers? His mother is having a hard time making ends meet, and I want to make sure he keeps his asthma under control."

"Sure did," Ada assured her. "Two of them."

Ileana gave her assistant a grateful smile, then turned and headed on to her office. From the moment she'd stepped into the clinic this morning, Ileana had been working nonstop. With cold weather still hanging on, the flu season was lingering with it. Patients with coughs, fevers and runny noses had been in and out of the examining rooms all day. She'd hardly had time to drink a whole cup of coffee, much less eat the thermos of soup she'd brought for lunch.

Her private office was small but nicely furnished with a large cherrywood desk, leather chairs and small matching couch. Along the outside wall, a bay window framed a partial view of Sierra Blanca. The area had gotten a record snowfall this year, and vacationing skiers had been coming into town in a steady stream to enjoy the fresh powder on the slopes. Ileana often found herself treating a myriad of injuries relating to the snow sports that went on in the nearby mountains, but so far today there had been no sprains, cuts or bruises, only systemic illnesses.

She'd just sat down at her desk and reached for the lunch she'd left waiting more than an hour ago when Ada suddenly appeared in the doorway.

"Ileana, I'm sorry to bother you again."

The odd look on the woman's face caused alarm bells to clang. Had something happened to a patient? "What's wrong?" Ileana asked as she started to rise to her feet.

Immediately, Ada motioned for her to sit back down. "No. It's not an emergency. Although, he sorta looks like one to me," she added coyly, then smiled. "There's a cowboy in the waiting room. With a bunch of flowers. He told Evaline he was here to see you. She pointed out that he didn't have an appointment, so he told her to put him down as a walk-in."

Mac! What was he doing here at the clinic—and with flowers? Was he planning to take them over to the hospital to Frankie? No. She couldn't allow that. The woman would want to know where they came from, and Frankie was still far from being strong enough to hear that her estranged son was in town. *If* he was her son, Ileana reminded herself.

Ileana twisted the plastic lid back on the fat thermos. "I'll deal with this, Ada. Please send him back here to my office. And hold everything else. Even my calls."

She could see questions rolling across Ada's face, but her assistant innately knew when to keep them to herself. Instead, the nurse simply nodded.

"Will do," she told Ileana.

Once Ada disappeared down the hallway, Ileana drew in a deep breath and passed a shaky hand over her face. How could she face the man after that kiss he'd given her? After she'd raced out of there like a complete idiot? Long after she'd fled the ranch house and even after she'd gone to bed, the man and her overwhelming reaction to him continued to dominate her thoughts. The only time she was able to dismiss him from her mind was when she was examining a patient. For that much, she supposed she should be thankful.

Down the corridor, a few feet from the open door of her office, she could hear his boot heels tapping against the red and white tile. The anticipation of seeing him again made Ileana's heart pound, then settle into a rapid flutter. Thank God she wasn't hooked up to an EKG. Her colleagues would take one look at the reading and suspect she had heart trouble. And maybe she did.

Quickly, she cleared her throat and smoothed a hand over her hair. By the time Mac and Ada appeared in the doorway, she was sitting ramrod straight, her face quietly composed.

"Here's your new patient, Doc. I'll be in the drug room whenever you're ready to see Mrs. Talbot."

"Thank you, Ada. I'll be there in a few minutes," she told the nurse.

Ada disappeared, and Ileana forced herself to focus on Mac. As he sauntered casually over to her desk, she noticed he was dressed in jeans and a hunter-green shirt. His cheeks were ruddy from the cold wind, and the scent of sage and spruce had followed him indoors. Tall. Tough. Sexy. The three images whammed her, tilted her off kilter.

"I hope I'm not interrupting too much," he said with a little half grin as he swept off his hat. "Your nurse said you weren't that busy. But I could see the waiting room was full. So I won't keep you long."

A huge bouquet of fresh cut flowers wrapped in red cellophane was cradled in the crook of his arm. When he extended them out to her, Ileana stared at him in confusion.

"What's this?" she asked inanely.

A dimple appeared in his left cheek, and Ileana felt the flutter in her heart leap into a gallop.

"These are for you," he said huskily. "I hope you'll accept them and my apology for my ungentlemanly behavior last night. I'm very sorry if I upset you."

Upset her! It was more like he'd sent her into upheaval, Ileana thought. But she wasn't about to let him know that. To do so would be admitting that his kiss had nearly made her swoon and turned her thinking on a one-way track—to him.

Struggling to keep her hands calm, she

reached for the flowers. "Your apology is accepted, Mac."

Deliberately keeping her eyes on the flowers, she folded back the cellophane. Her throat thickened at the sight of the yellow rosebuds mixed among pink carnations and blue asters. Other than her father and brother, no man had ever given her flowers. To think that a sexy cowboy like Mac was the first seemed incredible to Ileana.

"I hope you like the flowers," he said lowly.

She had to swallow before she could speak. "They're beautiful. But unnecessary." Lifting her head, she forced her gaze to meet his. "I should apologize, too, for racing out of the house without a word. I— It was just so embarrassing with Mother finding us... Well, you know."

She sounded like a flustered teenager rather than a mature woman and a doctor at that. But the man did something to her that she couldn't seem to control.

He smiled gently. "Yeah. I know," he agreed quietly, then let out an uncomfortable little cough. "I think I should tell you, just in case you haven't spoken with your mother, that I'm moving my things out to the Bar M later on. Chloe has invited me to stay at her home until this thing with Frankie Cantrell gets resolved."

Ileana was already floored just by him appearing here at the clinic with an armful of flowers. But this! Had her mother lost her mind? Only two nights ago, she'd been expressing her concerns about Mac's appearance ruining Frankie's life. Now Chloe had invited him into the ranch house as though he were an old friend!

Yet her mother could be very unpredictable, she thought, especially when it came to the needy. Chloe had often gone above and beyond to help people she'd never met before. This had to be one of those times, Ileana thought.

"I don't know what to say," she told him. "You and Mother must have had quite a discussion last night after I left."

He shrugged as though nothing earth-shattering had taken place. Ileana fought the urge to groan. She could only imagine her mother's response to witnessing their heated kiss. Oh, God, she could only hope that Chloe hadn't pointed out that her daughter was a lonely spinster in need of male companionship. That would be more humiliation than Ileana could bear.

"I tried to tell her that me staying on the Bar M might cause trouble with the Cantrells, but she doesn't seem to think so. I hope she's right. I've not come here to cause trouble."

Maybe he hadn't. But trouble was certainly brewing inside of Ileana. She could feel it coming on like a bad fever with no medical relief in sight.

"How did you find out about my clinic?" she asked. "Did Mother tell you?"

He shook his head. "No. I went by the hospital hoping to catch you on rounds. But the nurses said you'd already left. They told me where to find you."

"Oh. You didn't try to persuade any of them to let you into Frankie's room, did you?"

His grin was a tad wicked. "No. Do you think I could have?"

Ileana wanted to roll her eyes. Instead she pursed her lips with disapproval. "Not unless one of them wanted to lose her job."

His expression turned serious as he absently ran his thumb and forefinger around the brim of his hat. "How is Mrs. Cantrell today?"

"I ordered new X-rays of her lungs this morning, and they showed slight improvement. I'm feeling optimistic about her recovery."

"That's good." His gaze wandered over to the bay window and the view of the mountain. "I guess…you didn't mention anything about me."

Ileana felt something deep inside her stir—something far more than just empathy for his difficult situation. The raw need she saw on his face reminded her of her own disappointments and lost dreams.

"No," she answered. "I'm not sure how she'd react. I can't take that chance. Not yet."

Shrugging, he looked back at her. "I'm not sure how she's going to react, either."

He obviously had moved beyond wondering if Frankie was his mother. He seemed resigned to the idea that Frankie Cantrell and Frankie McCleod were one and the same.

He suddenly smiled and shook his head. "But I'm not here to talk about her. Will you be coming back to the ranch house this evening?"

The idea of repeating what had happened between them last night shot a thrill from the soles of her feet to the top of her head. She'd be lying to herself if she tried to pretend the man didn't excite her. But something told her if she expected to keep her peace of mind intact, she needed to give him a wide berth.

She gripped the stems of the flowers as though they were the last handhold at the edge of the cliff. "Not this evening. I have tons of work to do."

"Chloe tells me your father will be back home tonight. I'm looking forward to meeting him."

How could she resist him when he seemed so nice and unpretentious? Should she even bother trying to resist? "I'm sure you'll like Dad," she said. "He's an easygoing guy."

He awkwardly cleared his throat. "Well, maybe I'll see you tomorrow at the hospital."

She gave him a brief smile, while wondering why she didn't have the courage to tell him she'd stop by the ranch tonight, that she'd like to spend time with him.

Because men don't want those sort of signals from you, Ileana. You're plain and boring. A few minutes with you is all it takes to make them uninterested. Haven't they always dropped you after one date? Isn't that enough to convince you you're a disaster with men?

Doing her best to ignore the hateful little voice in her head, she said in the most professional tone she could muster, "Yes. I'll be doing my rounds in the morning and tomorrow evening."

"Okay," he said stiffly. "I'll try to catch you then."

She didn't make any sort of reply, and after a few more awkward moments, he gestured toward the bunch of flowers in her hand. "You'd better put those in some water. And I'd better let you get back to work."

Planting his hat back on his head, he quickly slipped out the door. Ileana looked down at the flowers and wondered whether she should cry or smile.

The next evening, after another long, arduous day, Ileana prepared to leave the hospital. On her way out, she stopped by the nurses' station to write out last-minute patient instructions.

As she quickly scribbled across the bottom of a chart, she said, "Renae, I want Mr. Tinsley's blood pressure to be checked every hour. And make sure his family doesn't sneak donuts or anything in to him tonight. I can't get it through to them that his diabetes will be fatal if he doesn't take care of himself."

"Doc, they think they're treating him when they bring him sweets."

She handed the chart to Renae. "Yes, well, I'm the only one who's supposed to be *treating* him," Ileana said firmly.

"What about Ms. Cantrell? Anything extra for her?"

"No. Just make sure she doesn't try to get out of her breathing treatments. I understand they exhaust her, but they must be done."

Her expression curious, Renae picked up the chart. "You haven't changed your visitor orders for her, have you?"

"No. Only Quint, Alexa or Abe. And only five minutes at a time. They understand why I'm doing this."

"Yes. But does he?"

Frowning, Ileana asked, "What are you talking about?"

Renae motioned with her head toward the waiting area. "The cowboy. The Texan. He's over there right now. I was expecting him to try to sneak down the hallway to Ms. Cantrell's room or something, but he says he's here to see you."

Ileana's heart picked up its pace as she looked down the wide corridor to where a glass wall separated family and visitors from the hustle and bustle of hospital traffic. From her position, she couldn't see Mac, but she had no doubt that Renae had spotted the man. Yesterday in her office he'd mentioned that he would try to catch up to her while she was on rounds. She'd not seen him this morning, and by this evening, she'd figured he would think it too late to drive all the way in from the ranch.

"Has he been here long?" Ileana asked.

"Maybe thirty minutes." Renae's eyes narrowed in a calculating way. "Just what sort of connection does he have to Ms. Cantrell, anyway?"

Leave it to the nurse to ask personal questions, Ileana thought irritably. Renae was mostly well meaning, but she loved to gossip. The last thing Ileana wanted was for the news of Mac's presence to travel through the staff and be repeated to Frankie.

"He used to know her. And I'd appreciate it, Renae, if you didn't repeat this to anyone. And that especially goes for Frankie."

Renae looked properly insulted. "You don't have to tell me to keep my mouth shut, Doc. I can keep secrets."

Secrets. If Mac's story was true, then it appeared that Frankie had been keeping some very deep, dark secrets, Ileana thought. The whole idea still stunned her. Almost as much as the man himself.

Shouldering her handbag, she said, "Thanks, Renae. I'll see you tomorrow evening. Unless I'm needed back here tonight."

"Let's hope that doesn't happen." The nurse's smile turned sly. "Are you going to drop by the waiting room to see the cowboy?"

Ileana bit back a sigh. "Renae, I'm sure if you'll look, you'll find you have plenty of work to do."

The nurse scrunched up her nose and giggled. "Okay, Doc. You don't have to say anything else. Have a nice night."

Ileana left the nurses' station and as she headed toward the waiting area, she unconsciously smoothed a hand over her hair. Normally she wore it pulled tightly in a ballerina's knot or clasped at her nape, but for some reason today, she'd allowed the dark, reddish brown tresses to flow freely around her shoulders. The unrestricted hairstyle had gotten several looks from her coworkers and Ileana suspected they were all trying to figure out what had come over her. Even if they had questioned her, she wouldn't have had a sensible reason for the change in her hairstyle. She didn't know what had come over her, either.

Mac was just ending a call to his brother when he spotted Ileana striding toward him. The first thing he noticed was all that burnished hair lying loose and shiny on her shoulders, and then his gaze caught the fatigue on her face. Apparently her day had been long and draining, and he could only wonder why a woman who was financially secure chose to work at such a demanding job.

Because she's a caring, giving woman, Mac. Because life holds a deeper meaning for her than it does for those women you've associated yourself with.

Irritated at himself for even comparing Ileana Saunders to his former girlfriends, he shoved the thoughts away and rose to his feet to greet her.

"Good evening, Ileana. Did the nurse tell you I was waiting to see you?"

She nodded, and like yesterday, Mac found his gaze going straight to her lips. He'd kissed many a woman in his time, and some of the exchanges had been sexual mindblowers. But none of them had affected him the way that Ileana's sweet lips had. The feel of her, the taste of her had continued to go over and over in his head like a vinyl record hung in one spot. He wanted to repeat the kiss. He wanted to see for himself if the whole experience had simply been magnified in his mind. If she was just a distraction from his other worries.

"Yes," she answered. "I'm surprised to see you. When you didn't show up this morning, I figured you had changed your mind about coming by the hospital."

An odd sort of excitement seeped through him, causing his lips to spread into a sheepish grin. He couldn't understand why this quiet, modest woman made him feel so very young, so happy to be alive. None of it made sense. But then, Mac wasn't going to try to figure it out. For tonight he was simply going to enjoy these unexpected feelings.

"Actually, I had selfish reasons for driving in from the ranch this evening," he told her. "And it wasn't to pester you about seeing Ms. Cantrell. I wanted to see if you were free tonight. To have dinner with me."

Her eyes widened, and Mac could see that his suggestion had taken her by surprise. The reaction made him wonder if she ever had social evenings with a man. Or did she put being a doctor first and a woman last?

"Dinner? With me?" she repeated.

"Yes. As good as Cesar's cooking is, I thought it would be nice to try one of the restaurants in town. And for us to share a little time away from your family."

She glanced away from him, while her fingers fiddled nervously with the leather strap across her shoulder. "I'm afraid I have to decline, Mac. I have lots of work to do tonight."

Mac wasn't used to being turned down, and Ileana's refusal chopped a hunk right out of his ego. But more than that, it disappointed him greatly.

"Do you work every night?"

"Almost."

"Then you don't take time to eat?"

She looked at him with faint annoyance. "Of course I take time to eat. I'm a doctor. I know I need nourishment to keep my body going."

He smiled broadly. "I'm glad you do. So it's settled. You have to eat anyway, so it might as well be with me. I've already told your folks I won't be back."

Shaking her head with surrender, she looked down at herself. "I'm hardly dressed for dining out."

The gray woolen slacks and thin black

sweater could only be described as practical rather than glamorous. But they draped her slender figure becomingly. In fact, in an odd way, the high neck of her sweater was more provocative than a plunging neckline. It teased his imagination and made him long to see what she was hiding.

"You look just fine to me."

She sighed. "All right. But it will have to be a short dinner."

Smiling happily, he took the coat she had tossed over her forearm and helped her into it. "Surely you don't want us to dine on fast food. That wouldn't be healthy."

Ileana could have very nearly laughed. Who was the man kidding? She doubted he'd ever had a second thought about anything he'd eaten. He was the sort of man who satisfied his wants, whether they were good for him or not.

So why was he inviting her to dinner? To think he actually wanted to be with her was crazy. She wasn't beautiful or interesting. She wasn't exciting or sexy. And as soon as Mac realized she was nothing but plain and practical, he'd disappear like mountain snow in mid-July.

"Since when have you been concerned about your health?"

Grinning, he eased his arm around the back of her waist and urged her toward the nearest exit.

"Since I met a doctor with pretty auburn hair and blue, blue eyes."

Don't get caught up in this, Ileana. The man has an agenda, and it isn't romance.

Chapter Five

Ten minutes later, as Mac drove them to the north edge of town, Ileana was still trying to convince herself that nothing about this evening was romantic. But it felt like that and more as Mac turned in to a small, rustic-looking restaurant built against a steep mountainside.

"I didn't know this place existed. How did you find it?" Ileana asked curiously as he helped her out of the cab of his truck.

For tonight the wind had disappeared, leaving the night air crisp and still. Mac's hand remained against her back as they walked across the graveled parking lot. She tried to tell herself that he was simply being a gentleman, but still the casual touch was creating havoc with her senses.

"I was driving around earlier this evening," he said, "trying to spot a nice place for us to have dinner. This one caught my eye. It's a simple little hideaway. But from the packed parking lot, I have a feeling the food is good."

So he'd already picked out a restaurant before he'd even asked her to have dinner, she thought. Did he think she was that eager for a date? That she'd be that willing to agree to his plans?

This isn't a date, Ileana. You haven't been on a date in years.

The little voice in her head had Ileana asking herself why she'd even want to go on a date anyway. The few times she'd attempted to find a compatible companion, she'd endured dates spent in boring silence, or she'd ended up exhausted from listening to her date drone on and on about himself. But she wasn't going to think about those times. This was different. She was simply having a meal with an acquaintance and nothing more, she reminded herself.

Inside the restaurant, a hostess promptly ushered them to a small table tucked in an out-of-the-way corner. After helping Ileana take off her coat and into a wooden chair, Mac took a seat directly across from her.

"I'm starving," he said as he slipped off his hat and shoved it beneath his chair. "I hope you brought your appetite with you tonight. I don't want to be the only one eating too much."

Earlier, before she'd finished her rounds at the hospital, Ileana had felt so hungry she'd been tempted to raid the vending machine and chomp on a candy bar between patients. But now food was nothing but an afterthought. Her whole body was buzzing, trying to digest the fact that she was sitting across from Mac in a cozy restaurant. Soft music was playing in the background, and he was looking at her as though he really wanted to be here.

"I'll try to down my fair share," she said with a faint smile.

He settled comfortably back in his chair, and as Ileana cast surreptitious glances his way she was reminded all over again at how muscular, rugged and sexy he was.

"So how was Frankie today?" he asked.

"Slightly improved. Her heart problem greatly slows her progress at getting well, though."

The idea that his mother might have a very serious heart condition left Mac uncomfortable. All these years she'd been away, he'd envisioned his mother as a vibrant, healthy woman. The way she'd been when she'd left their home. It was hard to imagine that same woman with thirty years added on to her age and in declining health to boot.

"Exactly what is wrong with her heart?" he asked curiously.

Her soft smile was apologetic. "I'm sorry, Mac. I can't discuss the details of a patient's condition. But I'm sure Alexa or Quint would be glad to explain it all to you."

Mac was about to tell her that he had no definite plans to speak with Frankie Cantrell's children, when a waitress arrived with menus. After she'd taken their drink orders and left the table, he said, "Can you tell me whether Frankie's condition can be fixed?"

Ileana picked up her menu, yet she kept her gaze directly on him, and Mac realized he liked her polite attentiveness. Whenever they spoke to each other, she made him feel as though she was really listening, as though what he had to say was important to her. He couldn't remember any woman who had done that to him.

"Her problem can be fixed. But she refuses treatment."

Mac frowned. "Why is that? In this day and age, medical procedures are a heck of a lot easier to deal with than they used to be."

"Frankie understands that. But I'm not sure what's behind her thinking. Losing Lewis, her husband, last year pretty much took her will away. But I shouldn't be saying this much to you about her health situation."

She dropped her eyes to her menu, and Mac decided not to push the issue. Sooner or later he'd meet Frankie Cantrell face-to-face and then he'd find out for himself what the woman was about. Or would he? Even if she turned out to be his mother, that didn't mean she'd want to speak with him, much less spend time explaining anything to him.

Dear God, what if that happened? He'd spent years trying to get over Frankie's rejection. How could he live through a second one? How could he go back to Texas and tell Ripp that their mother refused to allow them into her life?

Because you're a grown man this time, Mac. Because you've got a tough hide and an even tougher heart. You're not going to let any woman hurt you again.

Clearing his throat, he picked up his own menu and turned his thoughts to the list of meals.

A few moments later, after the waitress had served them wine and left with their orders, Mac said, "I met your father last night. I really liked him. He was nothing like I expected."

She warmed to his compliment. "What were you expecting him to be?"

He shrugged. "I'm not sure. More of a stuffy businessman, I suppose. He's very down to earth."

"I do have a wonderful father. Even though he has a stressful job, he's always put his family first. What about your father, Mac? Did you two get along well?"

For a moment Mac was taken aback by her question. Not because it was personal but because he'd never had a woman ask him such a thing. The women he often dated never initiated conversations about family relations. Their chatter was limited more to the latest movies, fashions or material things like cars or technical gadgets. At the deepest, the local town gossip was discussed. This sort of talk, especially with a woman, was very different for Mac, and he wasn't sure just how to go about it.

"We got along good," he said after a moment. "Owen was a very tough man in many ways, but he was devoted to my brother and me. All the years while we were growing up he worked as a farmer, raising corn and cotton. He taught us both all about making things grow from the ground and what it took to make a living from such a job."

So Mac's father was a farmer, Ileana mused. And from what Chloe had told her, Frankie's ex had been a farmer, also. The facts had to be more than coincidental. Her expression curious, she asked, "What caused him to leave farming and become a sheriff?"

"When I was sixteen, we went through a really rough period when the price of corn plummeted and cotton wasn't much better. Add a drought onto that and it nearly wiped us out financially. That's when Dad decided he needed a more stable income and a friend talked him into running for the county sheriff's position. Once he won the election and became certified as a law officer, Dad seemed to take to the job. Besides having a knack for solving crimes, he treated everyone fairly, and I think that's why he kept getting reelected."

"So you and your brother took to that side of your father, the law official part of him rather than the farming," she mused aloud.

Mac nodded. "Seems that way. Although my brother Ripp still likes to make things grow. And he's good at it. Now that he has a family I wouldn't be surprised to hear him say he's putting away his badge and going back into farming. But me, no. That's too mundane for me."

She took another tiny sip from her wineglass, then placed it on the table. "So you need excitement in your life," she said more as a statement than a question.

Shrugging, Mac wondered why her comment made him feel just a tad shallow. There wasn't anything wrong with wanting excitement. Everyone needed a little dose of it, didn't they? Otherwise life would be boring.

"If you want to put it that way," he said. "I guess I'd have to say I'd rather be shot at than sit in a tractor for twelve to fourteen hours a day."

Mac expected to see a flash of disapproval in her eyes and was surprised when he didn't.

"We all have a different calling," she said. "And yours is being a lawman just like mine is being a doctor. We can't make ourselves be something we're not."

The waitress arrived with their salads, and while she served them, Mac wondered if Ileana was really as understanding as she seemed or if she was simply being diplomatic. Once the waitress headed off to another table, Mac said, "Being a deputy is not a macho thing with me, Ileana. I like the notion of serving the public, of helping my fellow citizens remain safe in their homes and on the streets. If that sounds corny, I can't help it."

Across the table, Ileana forced an interest in the crispy romaine lettuce. But that was difficult to do when all she wanted to do was gaze at him, listen to his soft drawl and watch the subtle expressions move across his features. Being with the man was intoxicating, she realized. He made her forget who she was, what she was.

"I don't think it's corny. I think it's admirable. Remember, I've had relatives in law enforcement, too." She forced herself to chew and swallow. "So what exactly happened to your father? He must have died a fairly young man."

He grimaced. "Dad died when he was only fifty-six years old. He developed emphysema—a bad case. Probably from all the dust and herbicides he inhaled when he was young. That was before he could afford a tractor with a cab."

"That's so unfortunate," she said. "Especially when his illness could have probably been prevented."

"Yeah. But he did the best he could with what he had. And I admire him for that. Especially when I know he was working hard to put food on the table for his family."

The idea of this big, strong man losing so much, hurting so much, touched Ileana deep inside. Especially when she could see that he'd had the inner strength to go on and make something worthy of himself. "I can't imagine what it must be like to lose both parents."

He looked across at her. "When Dad died Mom had already been gone for twenty-odd years. Ripp and I had long gotten used to not having a mother."

Her heart winced as she tried to picture Frankie Cantrell, or any woman for that matter, deliberately leaving two sons behind. If by some wild chance Ileana ever had children, she'd make them the center of her world. Nothing and no one could separate her from them.

"So your father was farming when your mother left the family?"

Mac nodded. "My brother and I were both in high school when he became sheriff. And we thought having our dad as the sheriff was pretty neat. Until he got in a shoot-out with a bank robber and then we were scared that something would happen to him." His face was suddenly touched with a mixture of pride and irony. "We didn't know something else was going to happen to him and that it would have nothing to do with a bullet."

The waitress arrived with their main courses. Ileana promptly dug into the grilled salmon on her plate, while from the thick veil of her dark lashes, she watched him slice into a rare rib eye steak.

His strong, brown hands evoked all sorts of images in Ileana's mind, most of them so erotic that she was shocked at herself. Men had touched her body before, and though some of their touches had been pleasant, none of them had ever elicited pure desire in her, the kind that made a person lose all control, the kind that she'd felt in Mac's kiss.

Oh, God, she prayed, don't let me think about that. About the way she'd wanted him.

Clearing her throat, she asked, "So now it's just you and your brother?"

"That's right. Our father's parents both passed away about the time Ripp and I graduated high school. Mom's parents, the Andersons, never kept in touch. Mom never talked about them, and Dad once told us that his in-laws had disapproved of Frankie marrying him, so they'd always kept their distance. We never met them, so it's impossible to say whether they're still living or not." His face grim, he sliced off another bite of beef. "I had a wife once, too. But that only lasted a couple years. Now I'm content to let my brother be a husband and father."

The fork full of salmon she was about to put in her mouth paused in midair. "You were married once?"

A cynical grin twisted his lips. "Yes. Does that surprise you?"

Everything about him surprised her, Ileana thought. "Yes, it does. You—don't seem the sort."

"My ex didn't think so in the end either," he said wryly.

The idea that he'd once thought of one woman enough to marry her intrigued and bothered Ileana. In a fantasy world, she wanted to think Mac had never loved a woman before. That he would never love one in the future, unless that one was her. But she was a doctor, and she didn't deal in fantasies.

"If she didn't think you were the husband sort, then I'm curious as to why she married you," Ileana told him.

He chuckled, but the sound didn't hold much amusement. "Because she thought it would be fun for us to be husband and wife."

"Fun?" Ileana parroted. "Is that all?"

"Well, I think Brenna halfway loved me until I tried to make the marriage serious. You see, she wasn't ready for settling down and raising children, so she cut out."

Ileana gripped her fork. "What about you? Did you love her?"

His gaze dropped evasively to his plate. "I married her when I was twenty-five because I liked her a lot and we had fun together. I thought that was enough. It was a heck of a lot more than some of my friends had. But after a while I got tired of all the going and partying. I thought if we settled down and had children that it would change both of us for the better. I thought it would make me love her and she love me. I was young and green. I didn't really understand what marriage meant. It ended after two years."

"Well, we all live and learn," Ileana said. "And you seemed to realize the mistakes you've made, so why haven't you ever remarried?"

A grin touched his mouth. "It would take a hell of a woman to make me go down that road again. And so far I haven't found her."

And he wasn't hunting one, either, Ileana thought with a measure of foolish disappointment. Those soft, attentive looks he'd been giving her were probably practiced. If he even suspected she was thinking of him in a romantic way, he'd probably laugh himself silly. Only he'd keep his laughter inside so as not to offend her. He couldn't afford to do that when she held the entry key to Frankie Cantrell's room.

Feeling like an idiot for letting the man turn her head, even for a minute, she reached for her wine and took a grateful sip. Normally she never needed extra fortitude for any reason. But tonight Mac was shaking her up in ways she'd never imagined.

Lifting another bite of salmon from her plate, she said bluntly, "I know why you brought me to dinner tonight, Mac. And frankly, I should tell you that you're wasting your time and money."

His brows shot upward at the sudden change in her. "Really? I'm enjoying my meal. Aren't you?"

How could he insult her even more by appearing so innocent? she wondered.

"The food is good," she agreed, then her mouth twisted with sarcasm. "But you know what I'm talking about. I'm talking about your attempt at making it appear as if we're on a date or something. And the flowers yesterday—you don't have to do that sort of thing as a way to see Frankie. I intend to let you meet with her just as quickly as I think it's safe for her health."

Frowning now, he placed his fork down beside his plate. If any other woman had been saying these things to him he would probably be getting angry right about now. But this woman was different. She was like a hurt little kitten, hissing pitifully to ward away his advances.

"Look, Ileana, I don't know what brought this on. But you have me all wrong. This meal isn't some sort of charm tactic! It's insulting to me that you think it is! And I gave you the flowers because I wanted to. Because I'd hoped that you would like them."

Her head was bent, but Mac could still see the torn expression on her face. Clearly, she was fighting a war with herself as to whether to believe him, and he wondered why. True, she didn't know him that well. But as far as he could tell, he'd not given her any reason to mistrust him. Had some man deceived her, hurt her?

"If that's true...then it was a nice gesture," she finally mumbled.

Mac sighed as he wondered why this woman's feelings even mattered to him. "Ileana, have you ever been married? Or had a serious relationship?"

Her head jerked up, and she stared at him in stunned silence.

"I'm sorry if you think I'm getting too personal," he told her. "But turnabout is fair play, isn't it?"

Glancing down at her plate, she absently pushed her fork at a morsel of fish. "I suppose. But I don't know why that sort of thing about me would interest you."

Something in the middle of his chest was suddenly aching. It was an odd feeling that was totally new to him. He didn't know why the pain was there. Only that it had something to do with the woman sitting across from him and his need to make her feel better about herself, to make her smile.

"Why? Because you think no man could be interested in you? If that's what you're thinking then you're wrong," he said softly. "I'd like to know why you're still single."

The corners of her mouth turned downward, and Mac could see the expression of disapproval was aimed more at herself than him.

"Why? Because I'm thirty-eight and well-off?" she asked.

"No. Because you're a nice, lovely woman, and I can't figure out how you've escaped marriage for all these years. That's what I'm wondering."

A splash of color suddenly painted her cheeks, and Mac found himself enchanted by her modesty. Had Brenna or any of his dates ever blushed? But then Mac had usually associated himself with bold, thick-skinned women. They were easier to handle, easier to keep at an emotional distance. He didn't have to worry about their feelings, because there weren't many feelings involved. Ileana's fragility was something very new for him, and he felt like a clumsy-footed horse carefully trying to avoid stepping on a violet.

Her eyes met his, and he could see all sorts of doubts swimming in the blue depths.

"I'm sorry, Mac, if I sounded skeptical, but you see, I...well, I'm not used to getting attention from men."

She let out a nervous little laugh, and Mac could see the color on her face deepen even more.

She went on. "I mean...your sort of attention. I'm just a doctor, and that's the only way men ever look at me."

"Always?" he urged.

She slowly shook her head. "Well, I've had a few dates when I was much younger. But none of them turned into anything lasting."

"Did you want them to?"

A soft yearning flickered in her eyes, and Mac found himself desperately wanting to reach across the table for her hand. He wanted to fold it in his and let the pressure of his fingers tell her that he understood, that he knew what it was like to be rejected and humiliated.

"I don't know. I never got the chance to know any of them that well. I guess I'm not exactly an exciting date. I've always been a little shy, and becoming a doctor took years of schooling and training. I kept myself buried in my studies and my focus on a medical career. I felt confident and at home in a chemistry lab, but at parties I was a boring clam. After I finally accepted the fact that I was different from most women, I never bothered trying to catch a guy's attention." She gave him a hopeless little smile. "When God passed out brains he handed me a pretty good one, but I missed out on the beauty and personality."

"Who says?"

She shrugged, and he could tell his question embarrassed her even more. "Mac, my sister, Anna, and my mother are very beautiful women. Next to them I feel I'm lacking. But that doesn't matter. All I've ever wanted to be was a doctor. And I'm good at my job. That means everything to me."

Then why didn't she look happy and content? he wondered. Why was he seeing sad shadows come and go in her eyes?

"You've never wanted a family of your own?"

She glanced away from him. "I have my moments. Especially when I see my brother and sister with their families. But I would never want to marry just for the sake of being married. I want someone to really care about me. The way my dad cares for my mom."

When Frankie had married Owen, had she been looking for that same sort of love? During those years as a young boy, Mac had always thought of his mother as being kind, gentle and loving. She'd never raised her voice to her boys or her husband. But apparently she'd been unhappy. Had Owen not loved Frankie enough? Or had she simply not wanted to raise two rowdy boys? To Mac, either choice was not a pretty one.

Suddenly he couldn't stop himself from reaching across the table and folding his fingers around hers. "Ileana, beauty comes in all shapes and sizes. And I think those guys you dated needed eyeglasses."

Her cheeks were rose-colored as she demurely lifted her gaze to his and gave him a grateful smile. "Thank you for saying that, Mac."

Mac forked the last bite of steak to his lips while wondering what in hell was coming over him. It wasn't like him to be so protective of a woman's feelings. It wasn't like him to be so open and honest with a lady just because he had her out to dinner. Yet, he'd been telling her the truth when he'd said he had no agenda behind asking her out this evening. At least, not the sort of agenda she was thinking. He knew that Ileana was point-blank honest. If she said she would allow him to see Frankie soon, then she would. He didn't doubt that. And he wasn't trying to charm her into moving the meeting date forward. So what was he doing having dinner with her tonight?

Face it, Mac. You like the woman. She's soft and gentle and doesn't grate on your nerves. She knows how to have a conversation. And there's something about the fresh loveliness of her face that gets you, that makes you dream of quiet nights with her lips whispering in your ear, kissing you with love.

From out of nowhere he felt his throat tighten, making his reply little more than a husky murmur. "You're very welcome, Ileana."

Later, after coffee and dessert, Mac drove the two of them off the mountain and back through town to where Ileana had left her truck in the hospital parking lot.

As they traveled through the sparse traffic, Ileana was completely amazed at herself. For the life of her, she couldn't figure out what had made her open up to Mac like she had.

Why had she admitted to him that she'd always been a shy geek, that she wouldn't be able to turn a man's head even if she had him hobbled and bridled?

But, oh, God, the answers to those questions were nothing compared to the feelings rushing through her at the moment, the wild excitement bubbling just beneath the surface of her veins. She could feel her body longing for the touch of his hands, her lips aching to press themselves against his. This had never happened to her before, and she didn't know what to do, how to make it all stop or even if she should try to make it stop.

By the time they reached her truck, which was parked in one of the slots allotted for physicians, the parking lot was mostly deserted. Mac pulled up alongside her Ford, then cut the motor.

In spite of the wine she'd had with dinner, her heart suddenly started to pound.

"There's no need for you to wait around to see if my truck starts. It never fails. Besides, I can always find a maintenance man inside the hospital to help me."

Resting his arm along the back of the seat, he turned toward her. Streetlamps shed dim light inside the cab and caused shadows to slant across his strong face. She couldn't see exactly where his hand was lying, but she could feel its presence near her shoulder. The idea that he was so close to touching her left her feeling faint and foolish at the same time.

"I'm not worried about your truck. I only want to make sure you know how much I enjoyed this evening," he said.

Ruidoso hadn't seen a warm day in months, yet everything inside Ileana was melting as though he'd just yanked her into bright sunshine.

"I'm glad," she admitted softly. "I enjoyed it, too."

His dark eyes continued to roam her face, and Ileana unconsciously licked her lips.

"I don't suppose you're planning on stopping by your parents' house this evening," he said.

Her neck felt stiff as she wagged her head back and forth. "No. I have several charts to update before I head back to work tomorrow morning."

He grimaced. "Don't you have someone to do that for you?"

Ileana had never thought she suffered from claustrophobia, but the walls of the truck cab seemed to be shrinking around the two of them. His spicy scent was filling her head, his nearness making her breathing erratic.

"I could dictate comments and have someone else do it for me. But I prefer to do it myself. The well-being of my patients is *my* personal responsibility, not some person filing charts and records."

In spite of the dark interior, there was enough lamplight to see a look of appreciation flash across his face, and the sight pleased Ileana far more than it should have.

"Your dedication is to be admired," he said. "But it brings me to another question. Why do you want to be a doctor? Seems to me you're always working—even when you're home. Doesn't that get old?"

"Everyone gets tired—even at a job they love. I'll bet once in a while you even need a break from being a deputy."

He nodded in agreement. "The hours are crazy, and the pay is low. Not to mention the danger. And sometimes it gets so hectic that I ask myself if I'm crazy for hanging on at the job."

"But you keep on doing it, because, like you said earlier, you want to help people. It's the same way with me, Mac. I want to be a doctor so that I can help people."

He leaned toward her, and Ileana's gaze zeroed in on the lopsided grin on his face.

"Well, right now I wish you'd forget about being a doctor," he said softly. "There's still plenty of evening left. If you stopped by the ranch house, we could—"

"Mac," she gently interrupted, "I have to go home. Really."

His hand came up and stroked the side of her hair. "I was only going to say that we could—talk."

Ileana swallowed as her heart pounded wildly in her chest. "We've already done a lot of talking tonight."

His fingers left her hair to slide gently along her jawline before coming to a rest beneath her chin. "You're right," he murmured. "We have. And I've learned a lot."

Her lashes fluttered as her gaze sought his. "What have you learned?"

"That I want to kiss you again," he whispered as his mouth inched toward hers. "And I think you want to kiss me, too."

She tried to counter his words, but all she could manage to do was breathe his name, and even that one tiny sound was swallowed up as his mouth covered hers.

Her full lips were soft, softer than anything

he'd ever tasted. But it was their vulnerable quiver that got to Mac and urged his arms to circle around her shoulders. And it was the sweet surrender of her mouth that caused him to groan deep in his throat and press her close against him.

In a matter of moments he was lost in her gentle response, and then he was struggling, fighting the urge to deepen the kiss, to acquaint his hands with every inch of her body. In the pit of his belly coals of desire stirred to flames and heated his blood.

Knowing he was close to losing control, Mac jerked his mouth from hers and drew in a long, ragged breath. Beneath his hands he could feel Ileana trembling, her back rising and falling as she struggled to regain her breath.

Mac was stunned. He'd never expected to want this much, feel this much. Especially from a woman who could possibly still be a virgin, an innocent waiting for the man of her dreams.

He couldn't, in good conscience, be the man who burst those dreams. More than anything, even more than assuaging the desire simmering in his loins, he wanted her to remember him as a gentleman.

"I... I think we'd better head for home," he said with heavy reluctance.

"Yes—you're right," she said in a choked voice.

Avoiding his gaze, she reached to the floorboard for her handbag. While she retrieved it, Mac hurriedly left the cab and walked around to the passenger door to help her to the ground.

Once she was standing in front of him, Mac clung to her hand while his gaze snatched hungry glances at her face.

"I'll drive behind you until we get to the ranch," he told her.

"Okay."

She didn't make any sort of move toward her own truck, and Mac finally realized he was still holding her hand in a firm grip.

Quickly he dropped it and smiled sheepishly. "Would it do me any good to come here to the hospital tomorrow?"

"I doubt it. But miracles do happen."

He stuffed his hands in his pockets. "I'll be here then. Good night, Ileana."

To his surprise, she rose up on tiptoe and kissed his cheek. "Thank you, Mac, for the lovely dinner. Good night."

As he watched her climb into her truck,

Mac figured he had a goofy look on his face. Had any woman ever kissed him there before? Maybe. If one had, she'd not meant it. Not in the genuine way that Ileana had.

What the hell was coming over him, he asked himself as his gaze followed her retreating taillights. Since when did he let a woman end a date with a kiss on the cheek?

Since he'd met Dr. Ileana Sanders.

Chapter Six

The next afternoon, Mac was exploring the Bar M racing stables when he spotted Chloe on a nearby dirt track, exercising a big, steel-gray Thoroughbred.

After three circles in an easy gallop, she pulled up the horse and, after sliding to the ground, handed the reins over to a groom.

"Put him on the walker for ten minutes, Manuel, then shower him," she told the young man, who was using all his might to keep the energetic horse under control.

"Yes, ma'am."

Manuel led the horse up a slight hill to a big barn with a connecting row of stables. Mac continued to stand with his forearms propped on the board railing surrounding the race-track, until Chloe came within reach. Then he turned and tipped his hat politely.

"Good mornin', Chloe."

She was bundled in a red plaid jacket and her jeans were stuffed in the tops of her riding boots. The cold air had nipped her face with color, and the smile she wore as she walked over to him was one of exhilaration.

"Good morning, yourself," she replied. "What did you think about Rebel? Does he look like he's ready for the big track?"

Mac chuckled. "I'm the last person to be asking. I own a couple of horses, but they're quarter horses that I use to herd cattle. But from what I could see of Rebel he looked great."

She reached over and fondly patted Mac's arm. "I hope you're not getting too bored here on the ranch, Mac. I'm sure it's nothing like being home, but it has to be better than hanging around a hotel."

Mac shook his head. "I haven't been bored at all. The ranch is beautiful, and I enjoy watching all the horses."

Her expression turned keen. "Have you

spoken yet to Ileana today? I'm wondering if there's any change in Frankie."

"I haven't spoken to her today. But last night she told me that Frankie had slightly improved. That's all." Mac hadn't told Ileana's parents that he'd taken their daughter out to dinner last night. He wasn't sure why he'd kept the information to himself. He didn't think they would frown upon it; he just considered his time with Ileana private. "I plan to go to the hospital this evening and maybe catch up with her as she does her rounds."

Chloe frowned. "Why do that when you can catch up to her at her house?"

Mac realized that Chloe was merely being practical, but he wasn't at all sure that Ileana would appreciate him showing up on her doorstep. Even after that kiss she'd given him last night. "I don't think it would be a good idea to intrude on Ileana's privacy."

"Mac," Chloe gently scolded, "Ileana wouldn't consider you an intrusion. My daughter was born to help others. And I know she wants to help you resolve this issue with Frankie."

Help him? It wasn't exactly help he wanted from Ileana. When he'd decided that, he didn't quite know. He only knew that spending time with Ileana had somehow become more important to him than meeting Frankie Cantrell.

He was trying to think of a nice way to dismiss Chloe's suggestion when he caught the sound of approaching footsteps directly behind him.

As Mac turned to see who was joining them, Chloe said, "Quint, how good of you to come this morning."

The dark-haired man was dressed like Mac, in hat and boots and worn jeans. He was tall with broad shoulders and at least twelve years younger than Mac, but his rugged features implied a maturity that belied his age.

Quint. As Mac rolled the name through his head, it suddenly struck him as to where he'd heard it. This man was Frankie Cantrell's son! This man could possibly be his half brother! The notion nearly paralyzed Mac.

With an easy smile, the young man assured Chloe, "No trouble."

As her gaze swung guardedly from one man to the other, Chloe took Quint by the arm and turned him toward Mac.

"Quint, this is the man I wanted you to meet. Mac McCleod. Mac, this is Quint Cantrell, Frankie's son."

The whole situation felt totally surreal to Mac as he thrust his hand out to the younger man. "Nice to meet you, Quint."

"Same here," Quint replied.

Mac cleared his throat, yet the effort did little to ease the lump of emotion that had suddenly lodged behind his Adam's apple.

"I didn't realize Chloe had invited you here to the ranch this morning," Mac candidly admitted.

Quint tossed a fond look at Ileana's mother. "When this lady calls, I usually come running."

Well, Mac thought, Chloe had taken the question of whether to talk to Frankie's children out of his hands. With Quint here, he could hardly avoid talking about his mother—their mother. Oh, God, could this be any worse for both of them?

Yes, Frankie could be dead and then no one would know what really happened thirty years ago.

"Now that you're here, Quint," Chloe spoke up, "I have horses to tend to. If you men will excuse me, I'll get out of your way so you can get acquainted."

Both men watched the woman make her way back to the barn. Once she was totally out of sight, awkward silence settled in until Quint finally suggested, "Would you like to walk to the other side of the track? Down below this shelf of mountain there's a pasture full of yearlings you might like to see."

Grateful that the young man was making an effort to be friendly, Mac nodded. "Sure. It's kind of cold just standing here, anyway."

Quint smiled briefly. "Chloe tells me you're from South Texas. I guess this mountain air does feel chilly."

"I'm getting a bit more used to it," Mac admitted.

With mutual concession the two men turned to the right and began strolling along the outside rail of the exercise track. As they walked Mac was acutely aware of the younger man's presence, and for some odd reason it suddenly struck Mac that he was far, far from Texas, from everything familiar, from Ripp and home.

"I really don't know what to say," Quint said after they'd walked a few yards in silence. "The whole story that Chloe told me sounds rather fantastic."

"You're right. It does," Mac said soberly.

"Chloe says you have letters from my

mother and that they were mailed to a family friend of yours."

"I didn't know Chloe planned to say anything to you," Mac admitted. "I wasn't sure—I didn't want to concern you or your sister if this turned out to be untrue. But now that Chloe has let you in on part of it, you might as well hear everything."

Quint nodded. "I'd appreciate that, Mac. This whole thing is…well, it's pretty much shaken my sister and me. Hell, it's more than shaken us—we're both in a daze! And we don't know what to think…except that we've got to find out the truth about all this."

Mac let out a breath of relief. At least this man wasn't accusing him of being a crackpot or threatening legal action to keep him away from Frankie. Apparently, he must have recognized a thread of truth to Mac's story.

Mac said, "We only learned about the letters a little over two weeks ago. My brother and I were both shocked when Oscar Andrews, Betty Jo's son, brought the letters to us. You see, we…well, for thirty years we haven't known whether our mother was alive or dead."

Pausing on the rocky ground, Quint looked

at him squarely. "And you think Frankie, my mother, is that woman?"

"I can't think anything else. In the letters she mentions my brother and me by name. How else would she have known us?"

The younger man sighed as he shook his head back and forth in disbelief. "I don't know. It doesn't make sense. She's mentioned that she used to live in Texas when she was young and that she still had a few friends there. But she never went to visit. And she certainly never talked about being married before or having children. It's like—"

"She wanted to forget she ever had us," Mac finished for him.

Quint's jaw dropped, and Mac could see that the young man felt badly for him. Mac didn't want his sympathy. After all, they'd both been misled and the way he viewed it, Quint was just as much a victim as he.

Looking down at the toes of his boots, Quint said, "I didn't want to say it like that, but I guess it does look that way. I can't believe that Mother would just go off and leave two sons behind. She's not that sort of woman. She's always been dedicated to my sister and me. She—well, at times she can even be too clingy to her children. Does that sound like a woman who could walk away from two sons?"

Quint Cantrell's gaze was direct and forthright. But Mac was noticing far more than that about the man. His eyes were blue, the same azure color as Mac's mother. The notion struck him, crushed him with all the implications of having siblings he'd not known about. Of not having his mother's love while this man had been showered with her affection.

"From a law officer's standpoint, I'd have to agree with you. It sounds totally out of character."

Quint jammed his hands in his pockets, and Mac realized the other man wasn't wearing gloves or a jacket. Maybe that's why his face was pinched, his shoulders shivering.

"I guess Ileana has told you all about Mom's illness," he said.

"A bit. She believes in protecting her patient's privacy. But she made it clear that Frankie is too fragile to discuss this yet. And I respect her decision."

Quint regarded him thoughtfully. "I'll be honest with you, Mac. Mom's health is precarious at best. She needs heart surgery, but she won't discuss it. Ever since Dad died, it's like she wants to die, too."

"Have you tried to change her mind about the surgery?"

"Oh, yes. Alexa and I have tried. When we talk about it, she only gets angry. You see, when Dad died, my parents had been married for twenty-eight years. They were very close, and I don't think she's ever recovered from his death."

"My father died, too. About six years ago," Mac told him. "It's been hard not to have him around. Although, I can't imagine what he would think about his sons going on a search for their mother. He was very bitter about Mom's leaving. He practically forbade us to mention her name."

Quint looked at him curiously. "Why was that? I've heard of sour divorces, but that was carrying things a bit too far, wasn't it?"

Mac shrugged. "From what my brother and I can glean from acquaintances, when Frankie left her family, she moved in with Will Tomlin, a man who owned a tire business in town. We're not exactly sure how long she lived with him before she left for parts unknown. Only a few weeks, we think. Will moved away from Goliad County not long after Frankie did, and no one around town could give us information as to his whereabouts now. Anyway, back when all this was happening, Dad had to try to hold his head up while his wife flaunted an affair with a local townsman. It was rough on him."

Quint looked around him as though he needed to find a place to sit down. Mac understood the other man's feeling all too well.

"God, this is— It just can't be the same woman, Mac. The one appears to be exactly opposite of the other. My mother has always been a good, honest woman. It's impossible to believe anything else."

Feeling utterly terrible, Mac reached over and squeezed the other man's shoulder. "I understand, and I'm sorry about this, Quint. Maybe when your mother gets well, we'll find out that she never was Frankie McCleod."

Quint's expression was anything but hopeful. "Yeah, maybe. But I don't believe so. All I ask, Mac, is that whenever you do finally get to see Mother…be as gentle as you can be."

That terrible lump had suddenly returned to Mac's throat. "I'd never planned to be any other way."

Later that day at the Saunders Family Clinic, Ileana worked through the last of her patients, then made her way over to Sierra

General to wind up her workday. It was Friday, and this coming weekend she would not be on hospital call. Thankfully, a fellow physician would be handling her rounds for her. So barring some horrible emergency, Ileana's time would be free for the next two days.

Because her Friday patient list had been short, it was still daylight when she drove across the ranch, then up the mountain to where her log house was perched on a shelf that overlooked the Hondo Valley.

Eight years ago, when Ileana had turned thirty, she'd had the house built for herself. Up until that time, she'd lived with her parents in the main ranch house. And even though she'd always gotten along very well with her parents, she'd wanted to give them and herself more privacy.

Compared to the main house, the log house with its green tin roof was modest in size. But with Ileana living alone and with not much hope of ever having a family, she'd figured it had plenty of space for her.

Now, as she parked her truck and grabbed her handbag from the bench seat, she paused to gaze through the windshield at her home. The log structure sat snugly against the mountainside. Attached to the front, and shaded by one lone Aspen growing just to its left, a wide wooden deck with a waist-high rail ran the length of the structure.

Because of the steep terrain, there wasn't much of a yard. And since Ileana didn't have all that much time to devote to gardening, she'd left the rugged ground dotted with twisted juniper, yucca plants, choya cacti and clumps of blue sage.

Ileana figured the place would be too isolated and wild for most folks. Yet as she left the truck and climbed the steep wooden stairs leading up to the deck, she wondered what Mac would think of it.

The notion to invite him here had struck her several times today, but each time she'd squashed the idea. Even though he'd kissed her again in the hospital parking lot, she didn't want to appear too eager for his company. After all, she was wise enough to know that a kiss, even two, was nothing to a man like him. He probably went around kissing women all the time. She doubted a day passed in his life when he didn't have a woman near him. Ileana was nothing new or special to him, and she needed to keep that thought in her head.

And yet, she couldn't help but feel a bit

special, a bit hopeful about seeing him again. He'd implied that he might catch her on hospital rounds again today. But he'd not shown up, and she'd not waited around to see if he would. Renae had already been tossing sly questions at her about Mac. Ileana didn't want to add more gossip to the nurse's repertoire by sitting around the hospital, waiting for the man to appear.

She'd changed into a pair of jeans and a long-sleeved T-shirt and had just finished eating a bowl of stew when she heard a knock on the front door.

Figuring it was one of the family, or Cesar with a box full of leftovers from supper, she was totally surprised when she opened the door to find Mac standing alone on the other side of the threshold.

"Mac!" she softly exclaimed.

"I'm sorry if I'm interrupting, Ileana. I wasn't going to bother you like this. But your parents kept insisting you wouldn't mind. I just wanted to get an update on Frankie. I know I should have called—" Pausing, he grinned, then shrugged. "But I thought it would give me a good excuse to see your home."

Her heart beating fast, she pushed the door

wider. "Of course, you're not bothering me. Please, come in."

He stepped past her, and Ileana quickly shut the door behind him. Then with her back against the wooden panel, she took a second to draw in a bracing breath and collect herself.

"Just when I thought it was going to get warmer today, the wind starts blowing," he said as he shrugged out of his jacket. "I don't know how you folks get used to the cold."

"When you're born into it, you don't know anything else," she said, then walking around him, she reached to take his jacket. "Here, I'll hang that up for you."

"Thanks."

He gave her his jacket and his Stetson, and Ileana hung both items in a closet not far from the door. Then ushered him down a short hallway to the living room. With each step they took, she caught his male scent, felt his presence wrap a blanket of excitement around her.

"I'm sorry to say that Frankie's condition hasn't changed all that much. A slight improvement but not enough."

"Well, at least she's not worsening," he said.

As they entered the living room, she started

to invite him to take a seat in front of the crackling fireplace. But then she suddenly remembered it was dinnertime. "I just finished a bowl of stew. Would you like to eat something?" she asked politely.

"No. I had supper with your parents. Cesar is such a good cook that I couldn't down another bite. Unless it was dessert," he added impishly.

"In that case, we'll go to the kitchen," she told him. "I was just about to dig into a pecan pie."

Ileana guided him out of the cozy living room, through an open doorway and directly into a kitchen that seemed even smaller with Mac in it.

"Have a seat," she invited, as she gestured toward a round pine table situated near a glass patio door. "Would you like coffee, too?"

"Coffee would be nice. Black will be fine."

Ileana went to the cabinet and began to pull down cups and saucers. While she gathered the coffee and pie, she could hear him taking a seat at the table. Just thinking about him being here in her house, so near and touchable, made her hands tremble, and she silently scolded herself as she fumbled the pieces of pie onto small breakfast plates.

As she placed everything on the table, she carefully kept a polite distance between them. Yet in spite of that, she felt breathless and terribly foolish for reacting so strongly to the man.

"I suppose I should reassure you that I didn't bake the pie," she said as she took a seat across from him.

He chuckled. "Why? Are you a bad cook?"

She wrinkled her nose. "Not exactly bad. The things I do know how to cook turn out pretty well. But I only know how to make a few dishes. Mother says I always had my nose stuck in a test tube instead of an oven, and I suppose she's right."

As Mac dug into the pie, he decided Ileana was much more animated tonight. It was good to see, he realized, and even better that she didn't appear to be annoyed by his showing up on her doorstep.

After last night, when he'd practically forced her into having dinner with him, he'd promised himself that he wouldn't barge in on her private life like this. But he'd desperately wanted to see her again, and all it had taken was a little nudge from Chloe and Wyatt to put him on the road to Ileana's house.

Mac forced his gaze away from her face

and around the room. "I like your home. The outside is beautiful. And the inside is comfortable and homey."

Before he'd arrived here at Ileana's, he'd pictured her as having a modest brick or siding house with a neat fenced lawn that would grow flowers and green grass in the summer. He'd been shocked to see her home was nothing like that. Perched on the steep mountainside, the place was wild and untouched, yet simple and inviting at the same time. Exactly like Ileana.

Across the table, Ileana blushed at his compliment. "Well, it's nothing fancy. But I'm not fancy. Since it's just me I keep things the way I like them."

Her gaze flickered shyly up to his. "What is your home like, Mac?"

He swallowed down a bite of pie before he answered. "Nothing this fine. I live in an old farmhouse on a hundred acres. The furnishings are things that I gathered up at old estate sales, and the yard consists of one mesquite tree, two oleander bushes and a few patches of Dallas grass. Every acre I own is flat and the dirt black."

"Sounds like farmland. Is this the same home where you grew up?"

Mac shook his head. "No. After Dad died Ripp and I didn't feel comfortable around our old family home. Dad's last year there was pretty rough. Guess those images were too hard for us to shake. So we decided to sell it."

She smiled gently, and Mac wondered if there had ever been a mean bone in her body. He very much doubted it. He couldn't imagine her swatting a pesky bug, much less raising her voice to anyone.

"Well, I'm sure the place you have now is very nice," she replied. "Do you do anything with the acreage?"

He could see a true interest on her face, and the sight drew him to her just that much more. Which didn't make sense. Mac had always believed a set of flirtatious eyes and red lips were the things about a woman that caught his attention. How was it that Ileana's simple curiosity about his life made him feel so pleased and important?

"I have twenty-five mama cows with calves at side, one bull and a couple of horses. With my deputy job, that's about all the cattle I have time to care for."

She nodded with understanding. "So who's watching out for your livestock while you're here in New Mexico?"

"Well, where I live we're fortunate enough to have a warm enough climate that the grass stays year-round. So we don't have to feed much in the winter—just a few cattle cubes, a molasses lick and a bit of hay. But to answer your question, a fellow deputy is taking care of them for me."

"Oh." Her gaze dropped to her plate, as though she was embarrassed about asking him personal questions. "I can't imagine it not getting cold there. Does it snow?"

Mac chuckled. "Maybe once every forty or fifty years. Palms and banana trees and tropical plants like that grow where I live. Have you never been to South Texas?"

She shook her head. "No. I've been to Fort Worth to a medical convention but that's all."

Even though she'd shown a bit of interest in his life, Mac realized he was far more curious about hers. Which was something that continued to surprise him. Normally he didn't want to dig deep into a woman's psyche. If she had a pleasant personality that was enough for him. He didn't want to know what drove her. He didn't want to uncover the deep longings in her heart. But with Ileana, he found himself wanting to know anything and everything about her.

"That's a shame," he gently scolded. "You need to come over and visit your neighbor once in a while."

She put down her fork and picked up her coffee cup. "I don't have much time for travel. I don't like leaving my patients for very long. What about you? Do you travel much?"

His smile was a bit guilty. "No. I've only been to New Mexico once before and that was when I flew to Albuquerque to pick up a prisoner who was being extradited back to Bee County. Normally, the most traveling I do is driving over to Goliad County to visit with my brother."

"It sounds as though neither one of us strays too far from home."

"Sounds like," he agreed.

Rising from the table, she carried what was left of her pie over to a trash basket positioned at the end of the cabinet counter.

As she raked the scraps from the plate, she said, "My sister, Anna, lives here on the ranch so I don't have to drive but about a half mile to visit her."

"I've met her husband, Miguel. He seems like a genuine guy."

"Anna is very lucky to have Miguel. He

adores her and their children, a son and two daughters."

"What about your brother, Adam? Where does he live?" Mac asked.

"Only a few miles from here, but he comes to the ranch a lot. He and his wife, Maureen, have two sons."

Mac had been totally surprised to see her dressed so casually in jeans and a T-shirt. He would have never expected her to even own a pair of jeans, but now that he could see her in them, he was darn glad she did. The worn denim clung to her rounded bottom and shapely thighs, giving him a nice hint at the body beneath.

"Chloe mentioned something about your siblings being twins. Is that right?"

She placed her dirty plate in the sink, then rejoined him at the table. "That's true. Adam and Anna are twins. Did she also tell you that they're actually my aunt and uncle, too?"

Her question caused him to do a double take, and he shook his head in confusion. "Pardon me, Ileana, did I hear you right? Your brother and sister are also your aunt and uncle, too? How did that happen?"

A wry smile touched her lips. "It's a long story. So to make it shorter, I'll just say that my grandfather, Tomas Murdock, was a—well, a bit of a rounder. He got involved with a woman less than half his age. Only none of his daughters knew about it until my aunt Justine came home one evening and found baby twins in a basket on the doorstep."

"Oh, hell. That sounds like a movie or something."

Ileana nodded. "I'm sure it does to you. But it really happened. And because Tomas had died a few months before, no one knew he was the father. It took a while, but Justine's husband, Roy, who was sheriff of Lincoln County at the time, finally figured it all out. Turns out the mother of the twins was my father's sister, Belinda Sanders."

"Amazing. So were Chloe and Wyatt married then? How did they end up with the twins?"

"My parents weren't married, but while all of this was being sorted out, they fell in love and married. At that time, it was thought that Chloe would never be able to give birth to a child of her own, so she and Wyatt adopted the twins. Thankfully, I came along shortly after and proved that prediction wrong."

Finished with his pie, Mac picked up his coffee cup. "What about Belinda, the biological mother?" he asked with a thoughtful frown. "Didn't she want the babies?"

A sad shadow crossed her face. "Belinda had a substance abuse problem that caught up to her. She died not long after she left the babies at the ranch. Seems she became totally distraught after Tomas died. I suppose she wasn't emotionally strong enough to deal with losing him and caring for two infants."

"That's a hell of a story," Mac said, then immediately shook his head with regret. "I didn't mean that in a disrespectful way, Ileana, I just meant—it's rather incredible. I can't imagine what your family must have been feeling about the babies and your grandfather. Total shock, I suppose."

Ileana nodded. "It was a scandal that rocked the whole county for a while. But now—well, I don't bother explaining to anyone how my siblings came to be. I only told you because… you're trying to figure out things about your family in the same way that mine had to. I thought it might help you to not feel so alone."

He glanced at her. "I think you just explained why your mother offered to help me that first night we met. Chloe must have understood how I felt."

"I believe you're right about that."

His gaze studied her face, and he suddenly realized that when he now looked at this woman the word *plain* never entered his head. True, she wasn't painted with bright makeup, a chic hairstyle or flashy jewelry. But she had a quiet beauty that filled him with pleasure, a loveliness that wouldn't fade with age. Because it was a loveliness that came from deep within.

"So why did you want to help me?" he asked.

Her gaze suddenly fell to the tabletop, and her fingers fidgeted with the handle on her cup.

"I'm a doctor," she said after a moment. "Helping people is my business."

Now why did that answer disappoint him? Hell, what was he expecting her to say? That she'd taken a sudden liking to him? That something about him had touched a compassionate note in her? It didn't matter, he told himself. When it came right down to it, Ileana's opinion of him meant nothing at all.

Liar, liar. You actually think you can make yourself believe that, Mac?

Feeling restless now, Mac rose to his feet and meandered over to the patio door. Beyond the glass it was mostly dark, but he could see enough to discern that the mountainside was only a few feet away. He could see juniper and sage whipping in the wind, and in that wind fat snowflakes were flying and smacking into the glass in front of his face.

"It's snowing!" he exclaimed.

Behind him, Ileana left her seat at the table and walked over to where he stood.

"I didn't realize snow was in the weather forecast," she said softly as she peered out the window. "Maybe by morning you'll get to see a heavy blanket."

Her flowery scent and close presence was more than enough to distract him from the snowfall, and as he gazed at her warm auburn hair he couldn't stop his fingers from tangling in the tresses or his body from moving closer.

"I'd rather look at you, Ileana," he said simply.

He heard a little gasp escape her lips and then her head turned toward his. He could see uncertainty in her eyes, but he could also see longing, which was enough to justify pulling her into his arms.

"Mac," she breathed his name as his head bent toward hers. "This is all so new to me."

His lips brushed against hers as he spoke. "It's all new for me, too, Ileana."

Her expression dubious, she pulled slightly back from him. "But, Mac, you—"

"Yes, I've had a wife," he reasoned. "And I've had other women in my life. But none of them have been like you, Ileana. You're sweet and special, and I don't even know how to behave around you, much less treat you. All I know is that I want you. And I think you want me, too."

She emitted a groan that sent a surge of triumph through Mac and then suddenly her hands were resting against the middle of his chest, her lips were tilting invitingly up to his.

Mac closed the distance between their lips and wondered why his heart felt like it was singing.

Chapter Seven

A moment later, as the search of Mac's lips deepened against hers, the only thought in Ileana's head was that she was playing with fire. And if the flames got out of control, she didn't have a clue as to how to douse them. Or if she even wanted to end the consuming heat.

The warmth of Mac's body was seeping into hers, melting her in the most delicious sort of way. His lips were setting off tiny explosions that made her head buzz and her whole body tingle. Instinctively she snuggled closer while her mouth opened to the seductive prod of his tongue. When it slipped past her teeth and began to mate with hers, a moan of surrender vibrated her throat; her hands slid upward and curved around the back of his neck.

How had she lived so long without this man? Why had it taken *him* to wake up the woman inside her? The questions were racing wildly through Ileana's mind when the ringing of her cell phone crashed through to her senses.

Slowly, reluctantly, she broke the contact of their lips and stepped back. "I—it's—my phone," she said in a strangely garbled voice. "I have to get it."

She raced out of the kitchen, and, gulping in a ragged breath, Mac raked a shaky hand through his hair.

God, what was he doing? If the telephone hadn't interrupted them, he might have been on his way to seducing her. Is that what he really wanted? To make her just another one of his bed partners?

He shoved the frustrating questions aside as he heard Ileana answer the phone and begin to speak.

"Yes, I'm here. No. I hadn't planned on it. Codeine? No. She's had a bad reaction to it before. She's coughing because— Yes, I understand. But her heart is too weak."

There was another long pause, and Mac was beginning to wonder if she was speaking to someone about Frankie Cantrell, when Ileana said, "Tell her I'll be there in thirty minutes. Yes. Don't apologize. She's my patient."

As she stepped back into the kitchen, Mac waited expectantly while she snapped the phone shut and jammed it into her jeans pocket.

"I'm sorry, Mac," she apologized. "I have to go into the hospital."

It took a moment for him to digest her words, and when he did, he walked rapidly over to her. "I understand you're a doctor and that you have emergencies, but this—I guess it caught me off guard. And I—I'm selfish. Our evening has just started."

Her gaze clashed with his then awkwardly drifted to the floor. "I wasn't supposed to be on call tonight," she admitted. "But my stand-in is having trouble with Frankie."

The unease that raced through Mac took him by surprise. Whether Frankie Cantrell was actually his mother or not, he didn't want anything to happen to the woman. Not when he'd gotten this close. Not when his life and that of his brother's was on this precipice of uncertainty. And certainly not now that he'd met Quint. The man loved and needed his mother. For Quint's sake, Mac wanted her to survive.

"Is this something serious? Has she had a setback?"

"I don't believe it's anything physical. But I need to go just the same."

She turned and started out of the kitchen. Mac quickly followed on her heels.

"Of course," he said. "I'll drive you to town."

She tossed him a look of surprise. "That isn't necessary, Mac. I've made the drive at night hundreds of times."

Quickly, she opened the coat closet and pulled out a heavy woolen jacket. As she shrugged into the garment, she headed over to a small desk where she'd left her handbag and truck keys.

"I don't care if you've made the drive a thousand times," he said. "It's snowing, and I don't want you to make the trip alone."

She studied him for one brief moment, then held her palms up in a gesture of acquiescence. "Okay. If that's what you want."

"I do."

He grabbed his hat and coat, and they quickly left the confines of the warm house.

Outside the snowfall had grown much thicker, and the ground was beginning to turn white.

Even though Mac wasn't familiar with driving in such weather, he insisted on taking his newer truck. Fortunately, the highway wasn't yet beginning to pack, and all he had to concentrate on was following the unfamiliar crooks and turns through the mountains.

Across the console, Ileana wrapped her coat tightly around her and tried to gather her scattered senses. She wasn't quite sure what had just taken place between her and Mac. One minute they'd been talking and the next she'd found herself in his arms, kissing him, holding him as though she'd done it many times before.

In the dimness of the truck cab, her face burned at the memory of how she'd responded to him. And it wasn't embarrassment that was heating her face. It was the coals of lingering desire that were still warming her blood.

Clearing her throat, she said, "This is very good of you to drive me to the hospital."

"I'm glad to do it."

Why? she wondered. Where was this protective side of him coming from, and why did it make her feel so cared for?

She was studying his face, trying to decide whether to bring up the subject of that heated scene in the kitchen when he glanced over at her.

"I met Quint this morning."

His blunt statement took her totally by surprise. "Oh. How did that happen?"

"Your mother invited him to the Bar M."

Ileana bit back a groan. "And let me guess, she didn't let you in on it until Quint was already there."

"That's pretty much how it was."

Sighing, she said, "I don't know why she takes it upon herself to interfere in other people's business."

His gaze remained focused on the dark highway ahead of them, and Ileana wondered what he was thinking about her, their kiss, her family, everything. Never before had she wanted to get inside a person the way she did Mac. Sometimes he seemed so serious, and at other times he appeared to treat life very lightly. She doubted he'd ever revealed the true man to anyone.

"Is that what she does with you? Interfere?" he asked. "Is that why you don't live in the main ranch house?"

Ileana looked down at her lap. "She is not really an interfering mother. She cares—

sometimes too much. But I have my own home because I like the privacy. And my parents deserve to have their privacy, too. Especially after raising three children. But as to why she called Quint, that's just her way of saying I care and I want to help fix things. She doesn't stop to think that her meddling might not be appreciated at times."

Mac shook his head. "I don't mind. Now that it's happened, I'm glad I met Frankie's son."

"How did that go? What does Quint think about the situation?"

He shrugged as though the meeting wasn't a big deal, but Ileana figured deep down it had to have been rough on him and Quint.

"Naturally, he's shocked. He can't believe his mother might have kept a past life hidden. But he sees the evidence is a little too coincidental to dismiss. He wants to find the truth just as much as Ripp and I. I offered to let him read Frankie's letter that I brought with me, and he took it back to the ranch with him."

"What about his sister, Alexa? Does she know about this yet?"

He nodded solemnly. "Quint said he called her this morning. I got the impression that he didn't like giving her the news."

"Alexa is pregnant. I guess he didn't want to upset her unduly. But hearing that sort of thing from someone other than him would have been far worse," Ileana explained.

Frowning, Mac shook his head in regret. "I'm sorry, Ileana, about all of this. Sometimes—" Pausing, he glanced at her. "Sometimes I wonder if I've done the right thing by coming here. Sometimes I wonder if Ripp and I, and everyone involved, would have been better off if we didn't know the truth of the matter."

It was easy to see that he was agonizing over his decision to search for his mother. It was also obvious that he didn't want to hurt anyone along the way. As Ileana studied his strong profile in the darkness of the cab, she wished that things could have been different for him. She wished with all her heart that she could make it all better.

"Sometimes the truth hurts, Mac. But so does going through life with agonizing questions at every turn."

"Yeah. But it doesn't look as though there are going to be any winners here."

"I wouldn't say that," she pointed out. "You don't know what's going to happen yet."

He looked at her, and the faint smile on his

lips tugged at the very center of her heart. "Well, one good thing has come out of this— I met you."

Another flash of heat spiraled through her, and she forced her gaze on the falling snow in hopes it would cool her thoughts of this man who merely had to look at her to charm her.

"That's sweet of you to say, Mac."

After that their conversation turned sporadic as Ileana forced her attention on the worsening weather and Mac focused his efforts on getting the truck safely down the highway.

Thankfully, fifteen minutes later, they arrived safely at Sierra General. While Mac took a seat in the waiting room, Ileana fetched a stethoscope and Frankie's chart from the nurses' station as Renae gave her an update.

"Earlier tonight she was very restless. Her cough was worse, and she kept asking the nurses if her son had been around. And Annette caught her trying to get out of bed by herself. I know she's your family friend, Doc, but the woman is difficult. No, I take that back, she's spoiled rotten."

Ileana's lips pursed to a grim line. "I understand, Renae. Just do the best you can. If she's not having some sort of setback, I'm going to allow her to sit up tomorrow. Maybe that will help matters."

After a quick conversation with Jerry Vickors, Ileana hurried down the hallway to Frankie's room.

When she entered the small space, the head of the bed was raised slightly, and the television that was fastened to the wall in one corner was flickering a black and white classic movie. The woman's eyes appeared to be closed, but she must have heard the door swish as Ileana opened it, because she immediately turned her head toward the sound.

"Ileana," she said weakly, "what are you doing here?"

Ileana quickly walked over to her patient's bedside and reached for the blood pressure cuff hanging on the wall. As she wrapped it around the woman's upper arm, she said, "Dr. Vickers said you'd been coughing up a storm. I thought I'd better check on you."

Frankie's thin hand lifted from the sheet to wave dismissively. "It's that breathing machine that does it, Ileana. I told Dr. Vickers that, but he doesn't listen—" She broke off as a spasm of coughs shook her thin shoulders. Ileana didn't make any sort of reply as she pumped up the arm cuff. After she'd read the slightly elevated pressure, she said, "You tried to talk him into giving you codeine. You know better than that, Frankie. Am I going to have to put signs on your door warning the nurses that you're suicidal?"

The woman with blue eyes and black hair threaded with only a few gray streaks, frowned up at Ileana. "Don't be silly. I only wanted something to stop this damned coughing."

Ileana stuck a thermometer in her patient's ear and waited for the instrument to beep. "You wouldn't be coughing in the first place if you'd taken care of your heart condition months ago. In fact, you wouldn't be here in the hospital at all. You'd be home with your son."

Frankie closed her eyes as if to tell Ileana she didn't want to discuss the matter, but this time Ileana wasn't going to let her get off so easily. Frankie was her own worst enemy, and she wasn't stopping to think of the grief her stubbornness was causing her loved ones.

Another spate of coughing hit Frankie, but this time it was brief and not nearly as deep. "Ileana," she said after she'd caught her breath, "this isn't like you to be so mean. I thought you came back to make sure I wasn't dying."

Ileana bit back a groan. "You're not dying. In fact, I think you're doing better. Tomorrow I'm going to let you get out of bed for a while."

This news totally surprised her. "Oh, really? Is that why Quint didn't come to see me this evening? You told him I was better?"

So Quint hadn't shown up to see his mother, Ileana thought, and that explains why she'd been asking the nurses about him. Quint usually didn't let one day go by without seeing Frankie, and Ileana could only suppose his visit with Mac had left him too upset to face her. Dear God, it was going to be awful if Mac's appearance here in Lincoln County tore the Cantrell family apart. Especially when it wasn't his fault what happened thirty years ago; he'd only been a small boy.

"No," Ileana assured her. "I haven't spoken to Quint today. I'm sure he's very busy. The weather is turning bad, and he has plenty of cattle to care for."

Ileana warmed the end of the stethoscope in her hand, then placed it to her patient's chest.

"I suppose he gets tired of driving in to see

his old mother every day," she whined with a bit of self-pity. "He's young and has better things to do."

As Ileana listened to Frankie's heart, she wondered if this woman had truly left Mac and his brother behind, and if so, had she thought of them, longed for them? The whole idea troubled Ileana greatly, yet she did her best not to let it slant her opinion of her patient. She also told herself not to think of the sexy man who was sitting just down the hall waiting for her.

Satisfied with Frankie's heartbeats, Ileana helped the woman to a sitting position and placing the stethoscope to her back, focused on her lungs. After having Frankie breath in and out several times, Ileana straightened and cast her a firm look.

"Maybe Quint's tired of having a mother who refuses to help herself. Have you ever thought of that?"

Frankie sniffed. "Well, if that's the way he feels then he needs to say it to my face," she said, then sighed. "But at least he does show up. I can't say the same for Alexa."

If the woman weren't so sick, Ileana would have given her shoulder a good shake. "Alexa is hardly in any condition to be running up and down the highway every day between here and Santa Fe. You do want your grandchild to be born safely, don't you?"

For the first time since Ileana had walked into the room, a semblance of a smile touched Frankie's lips. "I can't wait for the little darlin' to arrive. It's the only ray of sunshine I've had since Lewis passed."

Hiding a sigh, Ileana reached over and pushed the disheveled black hair from Frankie's forehead. Under normal circumstances the woman was always fastidious about her appearance. Even at the age of sixty, she was very attractive, and Ileana had no doubt the woman could easily find another husband if she so wanted. But since Lewis had died, Frankie had simply been languishing in grief, and her heart condition was only complicating the whole matter.

"I'm glad you're happy. Focusing on something positive will help you get well more quickly."

"My children are all I live for," she murmured faintly.

Ileana studied the woman's haggard face and compared each feature to Mac's. Was there a resemblance? The nose? The cheekbones?

Carefully choosing her words, Ileana asked as casually as possible, "Frankie, did you, uh, ever want to have more children?"

The woman's brows puckered together. "What a strange question from you, Ileana."

Ileana forced an easy smile to her face. "Oh, the subject of Alexa's baby made the question cross my mind, that's all. Mom has always wished she'd had another child after me. I thought—well, you might have had the same sort of regrets."

Frankie turned her head so that her line of vision was on the picture window. Presently, the heavy drapes that framed the glass were partially opened, and Ileana could see the snow was continuing to fall at a heavy rate. Yet she got the feeling that Frankie was hardly watching the weather.

"I've often thought of other children— other babies. But I didn't think it would be fair to Lewis. A woman can't expect a man to take on more than he can bear." She sighed, then looked back at Ileana. "Are you getting the urge to have a child, Ileana?"

Ileana blushed. "Of course not. How could I be? I don't even have a boyfriend."

She reached up and patted Ileana's hand. "A woman can always dream, honey."

* * *

A few minutes later, after leaving Frankie's chart and written instructions at the nurses' station, Ileana walked down to the waiting area to find Mac in friendly conversation with an elderly gentleman and a young boy.

When he spotted Ileana approaching, he bade the two of them goodbye and hurried over to where she stood.

"Can you believe it? I found some vacationing Texans. The boy's dad had a skiing accident. They think his arm is broken."

His hand curled around her upper arm in a totally familiar way, and Ileana realized she was getting used to being touched by this man. She was even expecting it, liking it. Oh, God, what was she getting herself in to?

"How was Frankie?" he asked.

She swallowed at the tightness in her throat. "She's doing okay. Just being a bit fractious."

I've often thought of other children— other babies. Frankie's words whispered through Ileana's mind, and along with them came a haunting suspicion. But Ileana kept the thoughts to herself. Now wasn't the time for speculation. Mac had already been hurt enough in the past. He needed concrete proof, not assumptions.

"So it wasn't a dire emergency?"

"Thankfully, no. Are you ready to start back home? I'm thinking we'd better leave before the weather gets any worse."

"I'm thinking you're right."

With his hand at her back, they hurried out of the hospital. By now the wind had picked up and was blowing the heavy snowflakes in a horizontal direction. As they made their way across the parking lot, Ileana put up the hood on her coat and clung to Mac's arm to help steady her footsteps on the slippery ground.

Before they left the parking lot, Mac put the truck in four-wheel drive and drove the thirty miles back to the ranch at a slow and steady speed. Once they'd gotten to the Bar M, Mac gestured over to the main ranch house where a few lighted windows could be seen through the snow.

"Should we stop here? Or do you think we can make it up the mountain?"

She grimaced thoughtfully. "I'd really rather get home if at all possible. But if you'd rather not try it, I'll understand."

He allowed the truck to roll to a stop in the middle of the dirt road, then looked at her.

"Ileana, you know more about the driving

conditions. If you were in your own truck right now, would you drive it up the mountain?"

"Yes. Sometimes I have to stop halfway up and walk the remaining distance to the house. But it's not that far and I'm wearing boots."

Enjoying this surprising, adventurous side of her nature, Mac laughed. "I'm wearing boots, too. So we'll see how far we can get."

Ten minutes later, after a few slips and slides up the road to Ileana's house, Mac parked his truck safely to one side, and they hiked the last thirty yards. By the time they were inside, their coats were covered with snow, and they were both shivering from the cold.

"I'll stoke up the fire," Ileana told him, "after I hang our coats where they can dry."

"I can deal with the fire," Mac said as he shrugged out of his coat and handed it to her. "Just show me where you keep the firewood."

"Follow me," she said.

In the kitchen, on the opposite wall from the cabinets, Ileana opened a wooden door that led into a large mudroom equipped with a washer and dryer and a double sink. While Ileana shook the coats, and hung them on wall pegs, she said, "The wood is stacked in a little alcove just out that door over there."

Mac stepped through the door and found himself in a lean-to of sorts. Thankfully, the open side was facing the east, sheltering him and the stacked firewood from the driving snow. As he took a moment to glance out, he could see the mountain directly behind the house was now a white wall. Since he wasn't at all familiar with this sort of weather, he had no idea of how bad it might get, and he wondered if he'd be wise to hurry off the mountain or risk being stranded.

Who was he kidding? he thought, as he stacked several pieces of wood in the crook of his arm. If he was going to be stranded with anyone, he'd want to be with this sweet angel of a doctor.

Back inside, Mac carried the wood to the living room and, after removing the screen on the fireplace, carefully stacked it on the low burning coals.

He was using a poker to fire up the coals when Ileana appeared from another part of the house. She'd brushed her long hair and buttoned a thin sweater over her T-shirt. And if Mac was seeing right, there was a bit of new pink color on her lips. The idea that she might have used the lipstick for his sake made him glad. Which was totally ridiculous. Most women wore lipstick regularly. At least, the ones he knew.

But not Ileana. She wasn't the glamour, take-a-look-at-me sort of girl. He figured it had to be something special to make her put a bit of color on her face. And he wanted to believe *he* was that something special.

Smiling tentatively, she eased a hip down on the arm of a stuffed chair. "I'm sure you weren't planning on getting this much of a lesson about our bad weather," she said.

"That's all right. It'll give me a story to tell Ripp whenever I get home."

Home. Right now it was hard for Mac to picture the rooms of his house, to feel the emptiness that touched him each time he stepped through the door. It was different for him here with Ileana and her family. Just being around them made him feel as though he was a part of something. How could that be, he wondered, when he'd only known them for a few short days?

"You could call him," Ileana suggested. "He might enjoy hearing that you're in the middle of a snowstorm."

Mac shook his head. "I tried dialing him

earlier. I guess the weather has knocked out the tower signal. I couldn't get anything to work."

Ileana gestured toward a telephone sitting on a table at the end of the couch. "There's the landline. You're very welcome to use it."

"Thanks," he said with a half grin, "but I'll call him later. It's not necessary right now."

She rose from her seat and picked up the television remote lying on a coffee table made of varnished cedar. "I'll turn on the weather, and maybe we can find a forecast to tell us how much more of this we can expect."

The fire had begun to crackle merrily, so Mac put the screen back into position, then turned to see her searching through the channels.

He thrust a hand through his hair, then wiped it over his face. "Ileana, I'm wondering if I should head down the mountain to your parents' house. Otherwise, I might be stuck here tonight."

Her eyes wide, she glanced at him and then a bright blush stole across her cheeks.

"Oh. I didn't realize you were planning on going back to the ranch house tonight. The weather isn't fit for any more traveling. You really should stay here with me."

Chapter Eight

Utterly stunned by her comment, he took a few uncertain steps toward her. "When I drove you up here, I did it because I wanted to see you home safely. But I—well, staying here certainly hadn't crossed my mind."

She placed the remote on the coffee table, then straightened to face him. Mac was surprised to see her gaze didn't flinch shyly away from his when she spoke.

"Why not? I have a guest room. You should find it comfortable. Much more comfortable than traipsing through the snow again."

Mac could hardly argue that point. But staying here with Ileana somehow felt indecent. Maybe he felt that way because she was so prim and proper. Or maybe it was because his mind was drifting to places that were far from appropriate.

"I'm sure you're right about that." He rubbed his chin with his thumb and forefinger. "But what about your parents? They're going to be expecting me to show up. They're probably already wondering why I haven't."

Not bothering to reply, she walked over to the telephone and quickly punched in a number. After a few short moments, she began to speak, "Mom, it's me. Yes. I...that was our lights... I had to go to the hospital. Mac drove me. No. Everything is okay there. I wanted to let you know that Mac is going to stay here at my place tonight. The mountain is getting icy. Yes, we will. Yes, I'll tell him. Good night."

Ileana hung up the phone and looked at him. "She thinks you're doing the smart thing. And the snow is supposed to level off by morning. If necessary, Dad will send up a tractor to help you get your truck off the mountain."

"It does make sense," Mac said more to himself than to her. "I just don't have anything with me. Not even a toothbrush."

"I have a new one that's still in its box.

And if you're worried about clean clothes, my brother left a few of his clothes with me a while back to give to a charity in town, and I've never completed the chore. He's pretty much your size. In fact, there might even be pajamas if...you need them."

Mac grinned. "Thanks, Ileana, I might take you up on a pair of clean jeans in the morning. But as for the pajamas I wouldn't know what to do with them."

"It gets very cold up here on the mountain. As you'll find out tonight."

"I'll survive." Just thinking about her was enough to keep him warm, he thought.

She slid her palms nervously down the thighs of her jeans, then rose to her feet. "Well, I'll go make us something warm to drink. Would you like more coffee or hot chocolate?"

"Hot chocolate would be nice," he told her.

She gestured to the couch. "Sit down. Make yourself comfortable. It won't take me long."

"I'll just keep you company in the kitchen. If you don't mind," he added.

The corners of her mouth tilted upward. "I wouldn't mind at all."

Mac followed her into the other room, and while she pulled out milk and fixings for the drink, he walked over to the patio door and looked out.

"I can hear the wind howling out there," he said. "I hate to think of the wildlife and livestock having to deal with this brutal weather. Does your mother care for her horses any differently when it gets this cold?"

She chuckled softly. "Believe me, Mac, Mother coddles her horses at all times. Right now they're snug in their stalls. They're all wearing blankets, a barn heater is blowing and a radio is playing music for them. They're happy."

He turned away from the glass door and walked over to where Ileana was working at the cabinet counter. Her head was bent slightly, making her dark auburn hair slide forward to curtain her face. The few times he'd touched her hair, the rich, shiny strands had been soft and silky against his hands, and he found himself wanting to bury his fingers in them again, to gather them in his fist and draw her close against him. What would she think? That he was a jerk? Or would she be glad to surrender in his arms? Usually Mac could read a woman. But he was learning that nothing about Ileana was the same as other women.

Jamming his hands in his pockets, he said, "How long has your mother been interested in racing horses?"

"Since she was a little girl. From the time she could walk, my grandfather would take her to the track with him. So she caught the bug early on. By the time he died, he'd already taught her most everything he knew about training racehorses. Mother says she's one of those people who have been blessed with getting to do a job that she loves."

Mac studied her thoughtfully as she stirred powdered cocoa and sugar together. "You're doing a job that you love, aren't you?"

One of her slender shoulders lifted and fell. "Yes. But I don't think I get quite the same enjoyment that Mother does from hers. When one of her horses finishes at the top, she's jumping up and down, laughing and yelling. She stays on a high for days afterward. Now me, when I see someone pull out of a serious illness I just feel glad inside. That's all."

"Hmm. Well, it makes you happy just the same, doesn't it?"

She glanced up at him, and Mac was smitten with the way her blue eye was playing peekaboo with the strand of hair resting on her brow. The woman was sexy, he realized. And she didn't even know it.

"I suppose."

"Is there anything that would make you happier than being a doctor?"

Her gaze quickly fell to mixing bowl on the counter. "I've never thought about it that much," she said softly. "Maybe…having a child. That would make me very happy."

Yes. He could see where this woman might long to be a mother. With her soft hands and gentle, nurturing ways, she seemed made for the part. Yet on the other hand, he couldn't quite imagine her making wild, passionate love to a man. Unless, maybe that man was him.

What the hell are you thinking, Mac? Ileana doesn't want to make love to you. And she sure as heck wouldn't want a child of yours!

Why wouldn't she want a child of mine? Mac asked the pestering voice in his head. What was wrong with him, besides being a little arrogant and selfish and a set-in-his-ways bachelor?

Don't bother answering those questions, Mac. You gave up wanting children long ago. When you mentioned having babies to Brenna and she laughed in your face.

Ileana poured the cocoa and milk in a large pot and carried it over to the gas range. As she adjusted the flame beneath it, she said, "I don't know if you're aware of this or not, but Mother first met Frankie at Ruidoso Downs."

Her statement grabbed Mac's attention and jerked his mind off his meandering thoughts. "No. I didn't know that. What was Frankie doing there?"

"Working in the concession."

"So she'd needed a job when she first arrived in Ruidoso," he said thoughtfully.

"I think so. I remember Mother saying that Frankie was pretty down and out. She helped her find an affordable place to live and eventually a better job as a file clerk in a local savings and loan."

Mac crossed the space between them and stood next to her at the stove. "How did she meet Lewis?"

"Through my parents. They were giving a party for some of the local ranchers, and Mother had invited both of them. I guess you could say the rest is history. They fell in love and got married not long after they met. Now Frankie is shattered over losing him."

She must have adored her second husband, Mac thought, whereas, she must have hated Owen. Why else would she have left his father? He couldn't answer that. Not until he knew whether the Frankie lying in the hospital bed was one and the same.

"This is almost ready," she said. "If you'd like, you can find two mugs over in the cabinet next to the sink."

Glad for the distraction, Mac fetched the cups. After Ileana filled them, they carried their drinks into the living room and took seats on the couch.

For the next hour, Mac urged her to tell him more about the Bar M and her family. Eventually she pulled out a scrapbook of photos and pointed out special places and occasions that had happened over the years.

Mac was surprised at how much he enjoyed hearing her talk about simple family things, at how much her voice soothed him, seduced him into thinking the two of them were in a world all their own.

But eventually, she put the photos away and announced she was tired and needed to retire for the night.

Mac could have easily sat next to her all night for no other reason than to simply be near her, but he understood she'd put in a stressful day at work, not to mention the long added trip of going into town to check on Frankie. No doubt she was exhausted.

Rising from the couch, he said, "I'm sorry I've kept you up so late, Ileana. I wasn't thinking."

Standing on the hearth, she looked across at him. "Don't be silly. I stayed up because I've enjoyed talking with you. This evening has been special for me."

Special. Yes, that word kept coming to Mac's mind, too. And wouldn't his brother's jaw drop if he could see him now, enjoying a quiet evening at home with a woman who considered her brain much more important than her looks? Yes, Ripp would be surprised at this change in his brother but not nearly as surprised as Mac himself. Getting to know Ileana was something very new for a man like him. And very special.

Something suddenly swelled in Mac's chest, but he did his best to ignore the feeling as he gestured toward the fireplace. "Should I put more wood on the fire tonight?"

Ileana shook her head. "Once the fire burns out, the central heating will take over." She stepped off the hearth and walked over to him. "Come along, and I'll show you your room."

Mac followed her out of the living room and down a short hallway. At the very end, she opened a door on her left and, after flipping on the light, motioned for him to enter.

"It's been a while since anyone has stayed overnight with me. But I'm certain the sheets are clean," she said as she trailed behind him. "If you should get cold there's more blankets in the closet, and behind that door in the corner is your own private bathroom. And while I think of it, I'll go get you that toothbrush."

She hurried out of the room, and Mac walked over to the standard-size bed covered with a patchwork quilt done in bright blues and yellows. The room was spacious and comfortably furnished with plain pine furniture, including a rocking chair and a small cedar chest at the end of the bed. More photos of horses, the Saunders family and areas of the ranch hung on all the walls.

No doubt she was proud of her heritage and her home. And no doubt she'd never be willing to leave it.

God, Mac, why would that thought ever enter your head? Ileana is just a nice woman that you're getting to know. That's all.

But it felt like so much more when she returned to the room and his gaze encountered her smiling face.

"Here you go. I brought a tube of toothpaste with it." She handed him the slender boxes. "Everything else you might need should be in the bathroom."

"I'm sure I'll be comfortable," he said. Then on second thought he asked, "Will you be going into town tomorrow for your hospital rounds?"

Reaching up, she ran a hand over her hair, and Mac could see that she was weary. The sight made him want to scoop her up and carry her to bed, to stroke and cuddle her and then in the morning make breakfast for her.

"Thankfully, I'm not on duty tomorrow. Dr. Vickers will be on call all weekend."

"What about Frankie? You made a special trip in for her."

"I don't plan on doing that again. I've left certain instructions for Dr. Vickers, and he's perfectly capable of handling her illness while I'm off."

"That's great!" Mac exclaimed, then figuring that didn't sound quite right, he added, "I mean, it's good that you'll have time off to rest."

"Yes." She smiled faintly. "Maybe we could do something special together tomorrow."

There was that word again, Mac thought. Then unable to stop himself, his hand reached out to settle on her shoulder.

"Ileana, I—"

Feeling more awkward than he ever had in his life, his words broke off and her eyes widened in question, then flickered with something that looked to Mac like longing. Or was that just a mirror of his own feelings?

He swallowed and tried again. "I just wanted to say that earlier—before we drove into Ruidoso—that kiss…it was, well, I'd not meant for it to get so out of hand. But I'm going to be honest and admit that I'm glad it did."

He could hear her soft intake of breath, and then her eyes softened in a way that melted his heart.

"I'm glad that it got out of hand, too," she whispered shyly.

The urge to jerk her into his arms warred with his silent vow to be a gentleman and the violent tug on his emotions was something he'd never experienced before.

His eyelids drooped as he gently trailed his fingers over her hair.

"I think we'd better say good-night," he murmured. "Or I might not let you out of this room."

Her bottom lip quivering ever so slightly, she looked at him for long moments. Then finally she let out a long breath and nodded.

"Good night, Mac."

Slowly, reluctantly, he released his hold on her shoulder, and she quickly turned and left the room. As soon as the door shut behind her, Mac eased down on the side of the bed and tried to gather his senses.

What in hell was happening to him?

When Ileana awoke the next morning, sunshine was streaming through the bedroom window, and the smell of bacon and coffee was filtering beneath the door.

The fact that Mac was already up and obviously cooking had her jumping quickly out of bed and racing to the bathroom. When she emerged a few short minutes later, she pulled a pink chenille robe over her gown and hurried through the house.

When she entered the kitchen, she found Mac standing at the range, turning sizzling bacon strips with a long fork. On top of the refrigerator, a transistor radio was playing sixties rock, while on the dining table two places were neatly set with plates, silverware and napkins.

To have a man in her kitchen doing such things was a shock to Ileana's senses, and for a moment she simply stood in the open doorway staring at him.

He must have sensed her presence, because he suddenly looked over his shoulder and smiled brightly at her. "Good morning, sunshine! Ready for breakfast?"

Shoving her tumbled hair off her face, she walked over to him. He was wearing the same jeans and shirt he'd been wearing last night, only he hadn't bothered buttoning the shirt, and it flapped open to show a tempting strip of skin and chest hair.

If having him in the house wasn't enough to shake her up, the sight of his bare chest was. "Yes, I think so. Are you always this chipper in the morning?"

"Depends on how many beers I have the night before," he teased.

She rubbed fingers over her puffy eyes. "Well, I'm a deep sleeper, so I apologize for looking and sounding so groggy."

"You look very pretty to me."

The man had to be legally blind and in desperate need of glasses, she thought. The mirror didn't lie and yet Mac had a way about him that made her feel pretty and attractive, and that was something she'd never experienced in her life before.

Clearing her throat, she said, "Did you find everything you needed?"

"Eggs, bacon and biscuits. If you have some jelly to go with them, that would be nice."

Her brows lifted as she looked at the back panel of the range to see that the oven was baking. "Biscuits? You know how to make biscuits?"

He laughed at her dismay. "I found your dry mix. It was easy."

"But you have to knead them, roll them out and cut them!"

Laughing, he held up a hand in defense. "Sorry. I'm not that good. I just dropped them from the spoon. But they'll be edible."

Just to look at the man, she figured the most he would know about cooking was to open a can of soup or slap a sandwich together. He'd totally surprised her. Something he'd been doing ever since she'd first spotted him in Sierra General.

"I can't wait to try them," she said.

She left him tending the meat, and after

placing jelly and honey on the table, she opened the drapes to the patio. The mountain blocked out the sun, but the white coat of snow on the ground illuminated everything.

"Hey, that looks like a winter wonderland," Mac said as he placed the plate of bacon on the table. "Do you have a sled?"

"No."

"What about skis?"

She joined him at the table. "Yes. Put away in the attic. Do you know how to ski?"

He laughed. "Only on water. Remember, where I come from we don't ever see this stuff." He gave her a suggestive wink. "I'm trying to picture you as a little ski bunny with a stethoscope."

She laughed. "I put that away when I'm on the slopes. But it's been a long time since I've skied. I guess as a person grows older work starts to replace play."

"Unfortunately," he agreed as he pulled out a chair and gestured for her to take a seat. "Everything is ready, my lady. Just sit and let yourself be served."

Feeling ridiculously pampered, Ileana eased down in the chair and waited while he placed the rest of the food on the table, then served her a small glass of orange juice along with a cup of coffee. And all the while he moved about her, the only thing Ileana could think of was the way he'd kissed her last night, the way he touched her hair, the way he'd intimated that he wanted to make love to her.

Make love to *her!* The thought of it had kept Ileana awake long after she'd gone to bed and thinking of it now made every nerve inside her shiver. Would she be a fool for encouraging him? He would eventually be heading back to Texas. But, oh my, he was here with her now. And this might be her only chance to taste real love. To pass it up would be like closing her eyes to a beautiful sunrise.

They consumed the rich breakfast—and delicious biscuits—and then Ileana cleaned the dishes while Mac took a shower and changed into a set of her brother's old clothing.

He emerged into the kitchen just as Ileana was hanging a damp dish towel. The worn flannel shirt was just a bit snug, and she swallowed hard as her gaze traveled over his hard, muscular body.

"I'm all finished here," she said. "If you'll excuse me, I'll go get dressed, and then if you like we can walk down and check on your truck."

"Fine," he said. "While you're doing that, I'll stoke up the fireplace."

Hurrying to her bedroom, Ileana searched out a pair of jeans and a red, cable-knit sweater with a turtleneck. After jerking the clothes on and a pair of snow boots, she pulled her hair into a ponytail and swiped on a dab of lipstick.

Mac was waiting for her in the living room, and she fetched a barn coat and a plaid muffler from the closet before they headed outside onto the deck.

"Wow! This is spectacular," Mac exclaimed as they paused to lean against the railing and gazed out across the snow-covered mountains. "Too bad it isn't Christmas. I've never seen a white one."

Just having him with her felt like Christmas to Ileana. Excitement was surging through her, making her suddenly feel very young and carefree. She wanted to laugh and smile, the same reckless way her mother did whenever she won a derby.

She pulled on a red knit cap, then latched on to Mac's arm. "Come on," she urged, "let's walk down the mountain and see how bad the road looks."

The steep wooden steps were practically hidden beneath the deluge of snow, making their descent slow and cautious. Once they reached the ground, they discovered the depth of the white powder was over a foot deep and almost reached the top of Ileana's boots.

It took them a few minutes to make the trek from the driveway to Ileana's house, down the mountain road to where they'd left Mac's truck. When they finally reached the vehicle, they stared in amazement at the high drifts of snow piled around it.

"Do I have a truck under there some-where?" Mac joked.

"I'm so sorry, Mac."

They were standing close together in the middle of the road, and now Mac glanced at her.

"Why should you be sorry?" he asked, amusement curving his lips. "You didn't make it snow."

The morning was perfect with bright sun and no wind. The snow acted like an insulator, buffering the sounds around them, except for one lone cry in the sky. Ileana glanced up to see a hungry hawk circling the valley below. She understood the bird's lonely frustration. She'd lived it for most of her adult life.

"No. But I caused you to get stranded. And now you can't get down to the main ranch house. Unless one of the hands brings a bulldozer up here after you."

His arm suddenly snaked around her back and edged her closer to him. "Why would I want to do that?" he asked lowly. "Don't you think this is where I want to be? With you?"

She began to shake and her trembles had nothing to do with the cold. "I... I don't know, Mac."

With his eyes locked on hers, he curled his other arm around her waist and pulled her forward against his chest. Her heart hammering, her head tilted back, she watched the smile on his face disappear, his gaze turn sober.

"Oh, Ileana, you don't know much about men, do you?"

Her head swung back and forth. "I know how to treat one whenever he has an illness."

"Then I'd better let you know that I'm sick—sick to have you in my arms. Hurting to make love to you."

Ileana was too stunned to form any sort of reply. But then words didn't appear to be what he wanted from her anyway. Like the hawk she'd spotted earlier, his lips swooped down on hers in a kiss that was rough and tender, shocking and delicious.

With a tiny moan of surrender, Ileana flung her arms around his neck and pressed herself against him. Mac's hold on her tightened as his lips slanted hungrily over hers, searching, prodding, asking her for things she'd never been asked for before.

If she opened her eyes, she felt the sky would be whirling around their heads, or was it the center of her being that was spinning out of control? She didn't know. The only thing she knew was that she wanted to get closer; she wanted this man in the most basic way a woman could want a man.

She couldn't have guessed how long the kiss went on. But by the time he finally tore his mouth from hers, she was gulping for air, and her knees were on the verge of collapsing.

"Oh, sweet angel," he whispered against her cheek. "I never expected to want you like this. I never expected to feel like this."

"Neither...did I." She tried not to groan out loud as his nose nuzzled the stretchy fabric of her cap away from her ear and his teeth sank gently into the soft lobe.

His mouth nibbled at her ear, then tracked a moist trail back to her lips. After another long kiss that completely robbed Ileana of breath, she clung to his shoulders for support while her head tilted back and away from his tempting lips.

"Mac, we're standing in foot-deep snow! Don't you think we should go inside?"

For a moment he looked totally dazed and then a grin appeared and he began to chuckle. The sound was so warm and nice and infectious that Ileana immediately began to chuckle, too.

"I knew you had more sense than any woman I ever knew!" He grabbed her hand and began to tug her up the hill.

After several slips and falls that had both of them rolling and laughing like children in the snow, they made it onto the deck and into the house.

Once inside, they shed their wet boots and coats in the short foyer; then in silence, Mac took her by the hand and led her into the bedroom where he'd slept the night before.

Earlier this morning he'd straightened the bedcovers, and now he placed Ileana gently on top of the quilt and then stretched out beside her. As he gathered her to him, he could feel her trembling and felt his own heart hammering out of control.

"Are you cold?" he whispered against the top of her head. "Do you want to get under the quilt?"

She leaned her head back far enough to look at him, and Mac spotted something in her eyes, a forlorn plea that touched his heart, thickened his throat.

"I'm fine. I just…this is something I've never done before, Mac. I'm afraid I'll ruin everything. You'll be disappointed and—" Too choked to go on, she closed her eyes and pressed her cheek against his.

With a hand on her shoulder, he eased her back from him. "Ileana? My God, are you— are you telling me you're a virgin?"

A blush stung her face as her head barely moved in an up and down direction. Even though he'd suspected that Ileana had never had sex, he was still stunned by her statement, shocked to think she'd gone all these years without being physically connected to a man. And all he could do was stare at her as though he was seeing a different Ileana, one that was far too precious for him to touch.

"Please, please Mac. Whatever you're thinking—just don't laugh at me."

The anguish on her lovely face tore right through Mac. How could she ever think he'd want to hurt her in such a way? Had some other man insulted her innocence? If so, he wanted to kill him.

"Laugh? Oh, sweetheart, nothing about this is amusing. I'm—" He shook his head in wonder. "I'm thinking all these years—you've saved yourself for your husband."

Closing her eyes, she cupped her hands around his face. "In the beginning, when I was very young and romantic," she whispered. "Now, I—I've just been saving myself for the right man. And that's you, Mac."

Chapter Nine

Mac had never felt so humbled or special in his life. Nor had he ever felt anything so valuable in his arms.

Groaning with misgivings, he said, "Ileana, sweet, sweet, Ileana. I don't have the right to do this. And later, after I'm gone, you'll have regrets—and I don't want—"

Before he could finish, she lifted her head and pressed kisses on his cheek. "Now is not the time for you to go all gentlemanly on me, Mac. The only regret I'd have is if you go without making love to me. I'm not in my twenties anymore. I've waited a long, long time for a special man to come along and look at me. You're here, and I don't intend to let you leave before we are together."

And he couldn't leave, Mac thought. Hell, it would probably kill him if he tried to get off the bed and leave her now. Just having her sweet voice in his ear, her soft little hands stroking his face was enough to cause explosions of desire beneath his skin. Besides, she needed him almost as much as he needed her. He could hear it in her voice, feel it in her touch. The knowledge filled him with a power that left him trembling.

"I'm not going anywhere, my lovely girl," he whispered against her ear, then with another hungry groan, he brought his lips on hers.

Over and over he kissed her until Ileana's senses were whirling, her body twisting into fiery, agonizing knots. Need began to consume every inch of her, dictating her every move.

Desperate for any sort of relief she could find, her fingers reached for the buttons on his shirt and fumbled until she had the two pieces of fabric pulled apart and his hard chest exposed for the pleasure of her exploring hands.

As her fingers skimmed his heated skin,

she could hear the sharp intake of his breath, feel the tightening of his abs, and his reaction amazed her, pushed her reticence behind and emboldened her exploration.

Soon his hands were plunging beneath her sweater, sliding up her rib cage until his palms were cupping her breasts, his fingers kneading her nipples through the thin lace of her bra. But eventually the barrier of fabric became an offensive intrusion, and he broke the contact of their lips in order to lift the sweater over her head.

When her bra followed the garment onto the floor, Ileana had expected to be completely embarrassed by the exposure of her naked breasts. But there was such a tender, reverent look in his eyes that all she could feel was utter happiness, a need to give him more and more.

"You're so lovely, Ileana," he said huskily as his gaze devoured the picture she made lying against the patchwork quilt. "So precious."

Bending his head, he placed a trail of moist kisses across her throat, along her collarbone, then down the valley between her breasts. Each patch of skin that his lips touched sizzled like water drops on a heated frying pan.

But when his mouth finally settled over one budded nipple, the sizzles turned to outright explosions, and in a matter of moments she was writhing against him, silently begging him to make their connection complete.

When he finally lifted his head and looked questioningly down at her, she pressed her palm against the region of his heart. It was thumping rapidly against her fingers, almost as rapidly as her own heart was beating behind her breast. And once again, Ileana was amazed that she could have that much effect on this man. That she could actually fill him with that much excitement.

"Love me, Mac," she whispered breathlessly. "That's all I ask."

He drew in a deep, shuddering breath. "And that's all I want, baby. To love you."

She sighed, and then in a low, awkward rush, she quickly informed him that he didn't need to worry about birth control; she was protected with the Pill. "I—my GYN prescribed it for me—for reasons other than sex."

Smiling down at her, he reached for the zipper on her jeans. "Now you have one more reason for taking it," he said in a wickedly suggestive voice.

In a matter of moments he'd stripped away

the remainder of their clothing, and as he rejoined her on the bed, their arms and legs tangled like a moonflower vine waiting to bloom in the dark.

Mac's hands and lips spread magic over Ileana's body, stroking and touching, tasting and teasing. In turn, Ileana took her cue from him and used her own hands to express the needs that were crying out within her body. As her fingers explored the hard length of his muscles, raced over his feverish skin, she realized she didn't want to just receive pleasure. She wanted to give. She wanted to send his senses to the same height he was sending hers.

Yet when he rolled her onto her back and his mouth made a slow descent up her thigh, she was so lost in sensation that all she could do was grip the quilt in her two fists and wait with an anticipation that was nigh to painful.

"Let me taste you, Ileana," he murmured hoarsely. "Let me taste your sweetness."

Stunned at what he was about to do, she had no strength to protest, and then when his tongue gently probed at the intimate petals of her womanhood, any protest she might have had evaporated.

"Oh! Oh, Mac! Mac, I need you!"

She'd barely uttered the garbled words when wave after wave of incredible sensations began to wash over her. Her upper body strained toward him, and then her control slipped. Mindlessly her fingers dug into the flesh of his shoulders while she splintered into a thousand shards of glittering crystal.

Moments later, as she floated back to reality she was certain her body was incapable of feeling more, but Mac instantly proved that wrong as he shifted his position so that his mouth was back on hers, scorching her senses, stirring the simmering fire in her loins.

"I can't keep going, honey," he muttered. "I have to get inside you."

Wordlessly, she wound her arms around his back and urged him down to her. "I want us to be together, Mac. Like this. As one."

Mac's desire was already near the breaking point. But something about her voice caused him to rein in his needs. This wasn't just about him. Ileana was rewarding him with everything she had to give, and he wanted this time for her to be even more glorious than her dreams.

Cupping his hands along the sides of her

face, he bent his head and kissed her trembling lips.

"Hang on to me, my darling," he whispered against her mouth. "Hang on and don't let go."

He entered her as slowly and gently as was humanly possible. During the process he could feel her flinch and draw back. When that happened, he focused his attention on her lips, teasing and tugging with his teeth and tongue, while at the same time giving her time to adjust to having him inside of her.

When a moan of need finally sounded deep in her throat and her hips began to thrust upward toward his, he was sure the bed rocked beneath them. Stars exploded behind his eyes, and the only thing that existed at that moment was her soft, pliant body surrounding him, her eager hands racing over him, her lips pressing kisses across his chest.

The more he tried to restrain his thrusts and make it all last for her, the more he pushed them both over the edge. For Mac, time could have stopped or spun even faster. All he knew was that he suddenly felt her body tightening, convulsing, and then he had no choice but to fly straight toward the sky and burst through the clouds.

Mac was still trying to gather his breath and his dazed senses when he felt her faint stirrings beneath him. At some point his weight had collapsed on her, and now it took all the strength he could muster to roll to one side.

Even opening his eyes took great effort, and as he glanced over at Ileana he wondered what she'd done to him. Sex had never drained him like this before.

That wasn't just sex, Mac. You poured out a part of your heart to her. And you might as well get used to being weak because you're never going to be whole again.

He tried to push the thoughts away, tried to convince himself that this encounter with Ileana was nothing different. Yet as she opened her eyes and looked at him, he knew he was lying to himself. Everything about being with Ileana had felt new and earth-shattering.

"Mac."

As she breathed his name, the corners of her mouth tilted upward in a gentle smile, and Mac felt his heart melt like snow beneath a hot sun.

Her hand fell weakly toward him. He picked it up and hauled it to his mouth where he kissed each finger, then the middle of her palm.

"Ileana. Oh, Ileana." It was all he could say as he reached for her and pulled her body alongside his.

Ileana shyly nestled her head in the crook of his arm and closed her eyes. She'd never felt so utterly satiated, so completely content in her life. Mac had made love to her, and their union had been more than she could have ever dreamed or hoped that it would be.

"I'm so happy," she murmured.

His fingers meshed in the crown of her hair, then stroked down the long strands. "I'm glad that you're happy."

"Was I...terribly awkward?"

Her question must have caught him off guard because he didn't answer immediately. But then his brown eyes looked tenderly into hers.

"Awkward? Oh, honey, you couldn't have been more perfect."

She chuckled softly. "You don't have to overdo it, Mac."

Smiling seductively, his hand slid from her shoulder, down the slope of her rib cage and onto the rise of her hip. "You're one spicy doctor. And as soon as you give me a few minutes to recoup, I'm going to show you there's no such thing as overdoing it."

* * *

By the time they emerged from the house later that evening, the sun had melted at least half of the snow. Mac drove his truck up the hill and parked it in Ileana's driveway, but neither of them mentioned him going back to the Bar M. Although, as he shoveled snow off the front deck of the house and tossed it over the railing, the notion was following Mac around like a giant elephant.

What the hell did he think he was doing? He couldn't just camp here with Ileana and then in a few days walk away as though nothing had happened.

Why not? You've done it plenty of times before.

Damn it, why was he suddenly developing such a conscience? Ever since his giant mistake with Brenna, love 'em and leave 'em had been his motto. He didn't break promises because he didn't make them in the first place. He didn't expect a woman to love him. And he didn't want a woman to love him. His rules made everything easy.

But nothing felt easy when he looked at Ileana, when he took her into his arms and kissed her. Why did it feel so good, so right?

Why did the sky and everything around him seem a bit brighter?

A few minutes later, when Ileana came out of the house carrying an armful of crumpled papers and a box of matches, Mac was still asking himself those questions. But they weren't nearly as important as watching a smile spread across her face or enjoying this short time he had to spend with her.

"Do you like hot dogs?" she asked cheerfully.

"Sure. Why, are you getting hungry?"

"Famished." She gestured over to an iron fire pit sitting in one corner of the deck. "I thought we might build a fire out here on the deck and roast hot dogs for our supper. Unless you're too cold."

"Too cold! Are you kidding? This Texan is getting used to thirty-degree weather," he teased.

She laughed. "Okay, tough guy, if you'll pull the pit over here in the center of the deck, we'll get the fire going."

Mac positioned the large, bowl-shaped fire pit, then fetched wood from the lean-to at the back of the house. While he got the fire roaring, Ileana went to the kitchen and gathered the makings of the hot dogs.

Before long they were sitting on camp stools, roasting hot dogs over the warm campfire, while in front of them the evening sun was quickly dipping behind the mountains. Purple shadows were spreading across the deck, enveloping them in soft shadows. As Mac watched firelight flicker across Ileana's face, he couldn't remember doing anything so simple or pleasant.

"Do you do this often?" Mac asked.

She shook her head. "No. Adam gave me the fire pit as a Christmas gift one year, but I rarely use it. Sitting out here alone isn't— well, it isn't enjoyable unless someone is with me."

God, how many times had he sat on his front porch at home, looked out at his cattle grazing and wondered why it all didn't make him happier? Ileana had stated it simply and perfectly. It took two to make a place mean something.

"Yeah. I know what you mean," he said, then before he could stop himself, he reached over and clasped her free hand with his. "Ileana, we haven't talked about this. But now that some of the snow has melted I can drive back down the mountain to the ranch house tonight—if you want me to."

Her fingers tightened around his as she looked at him. "That's true. You can leave now if you want. But I...hope you want to stay."

Emotions totally strange to Mac suddenly swelled in the middle of his chest. "I want to stay."

Her shy smile was all it took to make him feel like the most special man on earth.

Chapter Ten

By Sunday evening it had sunk in on Mac
that in the past twenty-four hours he'd done
two things he'd not done since he and Brenna
had divorced nearly fifteen years ago. He'd
stayed all night in a woman's bed. And he'd
gone to church with her.

Maybe to most men those things didn't
sound like life-changing events, but the more
Mac chewed on it, the more he recognized
that Ileana was changing him. *Had* changed
him. Where was it all going to lead? How
was he going to go back to Texas and be the
Mac he used to be? Could he go back to being
that man?

There couldn't be any question about that, he thought, as he sat at Ileana's dining table, sipping at a cup of coffee that had grown cool while he waited for her to finish a few business calls. He had to go back to Bee County, and the sooner he did, the sooner he'd remember who he was, what he was. He'd get his life back to normal.

"I'm sorry about that, Mac," Ileana said a moment later as she stepped into the kitchen. "Dr. Vickers had several things to go over with me."

After church this morning, Ileana had changed into a pair of jeans and a striped shirt. Now as she moved over to the cabinet counter, Mac's gaze traveled appreciatively over the thrust of her breasts, the curve of her bottom and the shape of her thighs. Just looking at her filled him with visions of creamy skin and rosy nipples, teased his senses with the scent of lilac and the warmth of her soft body.

He clutched the cold cup while wondering why his desire for the woman never seemed to be quenched. "Problems?"

Smiling, she said, "No. In fact, he says that over the past two days Frankie has made a big stride toward getting well. Once she was finally able to sit up for an extended time, it's greatly helped her lungs."

Frankie was getting better. That meant he would soon be able to visit with the woman. And no matter how that visit turned out, his time here in New Mexico would end. Only moments earlier, he'd been telling himself he needed to go home. So Ileana's news should have thrilled him. Instead, his insides felt like lead weights.

"That's good. And your other patients?"

She poured herself a cup of coffee and joined him at the table. "I'll be able to release two of them tomorrow. The rest are coming along nicely."

He tried to smile, tried to hide the warring emotions inside him. "It must make you feel great to know that you're getting people back on their feet," he said.

With a modest smile, she reached across the table and covered his hand with hers. Everything in Mac wanted to turn his hand over and snatch a hold on her wrist. He wanted to lead her to the bedroom, make love to her and block out the notion that it would be the very last time.

Gently, she said, "And it must make you feel good to keep people safe."

He shrugged. "What I do isn't nearly as important as your job."

She frowned. "How do you think life would be for the citizens in your county if there was no law enforcement there? It would be dangerous and violent, that's how. People would have to alter their lives just to remain safe." A smile chased away her frown. "We all have a purpose, Mac."

Sighing heavily, he pulled his hand away and rose from the table. Looking at her hurt. Touching her hurt. Everything inside him was twisting with agony. It shouldn't be this way, he thought. Being with Ileana, no matter how short the time, should be making him happy.

Blindly, he moved over to the patio door and pretended an interest in the view of the mountain. "I guess you're right. And right now my purpose is to find my mother. Have you decided when I might see her?" he asked dully.

A long stretch of silence passed, and Mac figured he'd caught her off guard. For the past two days they'd not been discussing Frankie or the reason Mac had come to Lincoln County. They'd simply been enjoying the moment, taking pleasure in each other.

But now his question had jerked them both back to reality.

"I hadn't thought about it, Mac. But if things are still okay by tomorrow, I suppose you can see her then."

Her answer was like an electrical jolt, and his head jerked around just in time to see her rising from her chair and moving toward him.

"Tomorrow? Are you serious?"

"Yes."

Pausing in front of him, Mac could see her features were pinched, and when she placed her hand on his arm, he felt his heart crack.

"Are you that desperate to leave?" she asked.

He swallowed at the strange tightening in his throat. "No. Not exactly. I just…well… time has been marching on, and I'm…expected back at my deputy duties soon."

That was only a partial truth. But Mac didn't want to admit to this woman that he was a coward, that he was afraid to stay much longer, afraid if he remained in her presence he would end up doing something stupid. Like fall in love with her.

She appeared to be weighing his every word as her gaze wandered over his face. Mac could only wonder what she was thinking.

That he'd been using her? Oh, God, nothing could be further from the truth. Somehow he had to make her understand that.

"I see. I'm sorry, Mac. I wasn't thinking. I guess I was being selfish and thinking—" She paused, then released a long, shaky breath. "I've been…this time with you has been so special for me. It was easy to forget that you have a life back in Texas."

Summoning all the strength he could find, he made himself play it light. After all, there was nothing serious between them, just mutual attraction and respect. She wasn't expecting more and neither was he, he assured himself.

"It's been special for me, too, Ileana."

Her fingers tightened on his arm and like a man gripping a lifeline, he felt his strength slipping, his resistance collapsing.

"You are going to stay with me tonight, aren't you?"

The sweet innocence to her question, the gentle plea on her face was more than Mac could bear. Emitting a groan of surrender, he drew her into the circle of his arms and buried his face in the side of her silky hair.

"Of course I'm going to stay," he said in a muffled voice.

"I'll have to get up very early to leave for work," she warned him.

His hands roamed her back, treasured the feel of her warm body. "Then I'll get up very early and make breakfast. The least I can do is see that the doctor maintains her nutrition."

Tilting her head back, she smiled at him. "I'm holding you to that promise."

By midmorning the next day, Ileana was knee-deep in work yet having a heck of a time trying to concentrate on anything. Minutes ago she'd called Mac's cell phone and informed him that Frankie would be in her room and that he could go in to see her as long as he kept the meeting limited to ten minutes.

The realization that Mac was finally going to get answers to questions about his mother had left Ileana more than anxious. Several times this morning she'd dropped things, missed words in conversations and forgotten to return phone calls. If it hadn't been for Ada following her around, taking care of her missteps, she'd be in a mess.

Actually, Ileana was already in a mess, she just didn't want to admit it to herself or anyone else. She'd blindly stepped into Mac's arms because she'd been attracted to him, drawn to him in a way that she'd never been drawn to any man. She'd known their time together was temporary yet she'd plowed ahead, eager to snatch a taste of womanhood.

She'd not expected his lovemaking to make such an incredible change in her life. She felt different. She was different. Now, all she could think was that their time together was narrowing down and by allowing him to see Frankie she was speeding up the process.

Oh, God, what was it going to be like once Mac went back to Texas? Her house, her life was going to be so empty. Could she live on just the memories he left behind?

"Doc, are you coming down with something?" Ada asked.

Pulling her hand away from her forehead, Ileana looked up to see the nurse walking into her office. As Ada frowned with concern, Ileana straightened her slumped shoulders.

"Not at all. I'm just a bit distracted this morning."

"A bit!" Ada exclaimed as she rested a hip on the corner of Ileana's desk. "I've never seen you like this!"

Thrusting a hand through her hair, Ileana looked at the other woman. "Mac is going to visit with Frankie this morning. And I'm worried about both of them."

Ileana had given the nurse a brief account of why Mac had come to Ruidoso and why he believed Frankie might be his mother. Since then Ileana hadn't given the woman any hint that she'd gotten close to the man. Even though the nurse hadn't said as much to her, Ileana somehow sensed that Ada believed she was falling for the Texan.

"What do you think might come of this meeting?" Ada asked.

Ileana picked up a pen and began twisting it between her fingers. "I honestly don't know. I just fear that both of them might be hurt."

"Well, you can order the man not to see her."

"No. That wouldn't help matters. This meeting has to happen—for both of their sakes. I only wish—" Pausing, she let out a heavy sigh. "That I could see a happy ending out of this. For both of them."

Ada studied her keenly. "You've changed since he came to town, Doc."

Ada couldn't imagine just how much she had changed, Ileana thought. She was now a woman who understood what it meant to make love to a man, experience the rush of pleasure, the ecstasy of being wanted. Oh, yes, she'd changed. She just hadn't realized it showed.

"Just because I've worn a few dresses and put on some lipstick?" she lightly teased. "Come on, Ada, I'm still the same boring doctor you've always known."

"You're not boring. You never were. But you're more interesting now, and it's obvious the change has a great deal to do with your tall Texan."

"He's hardly mine," Ileana muttered, but even as she said the words her cheeks turned bright pink. "And we'd better get back to work."

Rising from her seat, she expected Ada to follow her out of the office. When the nurse failed to make a move, Ileana looked back at her.

"Are you stuck to that desk?"

Shaking her head, Ada smiled. "We've seen the last patient for this morning. It's almost time for lunch, or hadn't you noticed."

Amazed that she'd been in such a fog, Ileana glanced at her watch. "I guess time got away from me," she mumbled.

"Why don't you go over to Sierra General?" Ada suggested. "Maybe Mac is still there."

Ileana's eyes widened. "Mr. Hampton was the last patient?"

Ada nodded. "I told you that when we left the examining room, but I guess you weren't listening."

"Sorry, Ada. I've not been myself this morning." She hurried over to a hall tree where her coat and muffler were hanging. "I think I will go to the hospital. I'll see you after lunch."

Across town, Mac didn't know what to expect when he walked into Frankie Cantrell's hospital room, but one thing was for sure, he didn't expect to find the beautiful, fragile woman sitting in an armchair.

Her image was framed by a picture window, and the sunlight illuminated her face. As he grew nearer, Mac decided she looked much younger than he imagined, but much older than the woman who'd walked away from the McCleod farm nearly thirty years ago.

"Ms. Cantrell?"

The faint smile on her face told him that she didn't have a clue who he was. The fact hit him almost as hard as the sight of her. Yet he told himself that there was no way she could connect his image with that of a ten-year-old boy. One that she'd not seen in years.

"Yes. Are you the visitor that the nurse told me about?"

"I am." Bending forward, he offered her his hand. "I've been here in Lincoln County for the past several days, waiting for you to get better. Ileana—I mean—Dr. Sanders tells me that you've been very ill."

"Yes. But I'm much better now."

She politely shook his hand, and Mac noticed her fingers were cool, the skin as delicate as a rose petal. The blue of her eyes was deep, and while they curiously scanned his face, Mac could only think how her brow and the shape of her mouth resembled his brother. Dear God, if there had been any question before, there wasn't now. This was their mother! His mother!

"You say you've been waiting for me to get well? I'm sorry but you have the advantage on me. Should I know you, young man?"

His nostrils flared as he drew in a deep breath, and unexpected pain burned in the middle of his chest.

"I think so. My name is Phineas. Phineas McCleod. But I used to be Mac to you."

All these years Mac had dreamed of this moment. He'd imagined finding his mother and how she would look once he confronted her. He'd believed that shocking her would give him pleasure. It didn't.

Her face not only appeared ashen but it looked wounded. As though he'd physically struck her with his open hand.

"Mac."

She repeated his name in childlike wonder, as though she'd just stepped into a dream world.

"Yes."

Her mouth fell open, and one hand clutched her throat. For a moment he feared the shock was going to give her a heart attack, but then she seemed to gather herself, and he was relieved to see a bit of color flood back into her cheeks.

"How did you find me?" she finally asked.

"Betty Jo Andrews. She died. Or did you know?"

Her expression sober, she nodded. "Yes," she said hoarsely. "I keep up with Goliad County obits."

Then obviously she knew that her first

husband had died nearly seven years ago. Yet she'd not shown her face to her sons. Not bothered to acknowledge their father's death. What had happened to this woman? he wondered incredulously. How could she have gone from a loving, devoted mother, to denying her own sons?

"Oscar, her son, gave the correspondence you'd exchanged with Betty Jo to Ripp."

"Ripp. How is he?"

"He's fine. He's married now. With a family."

"That's good." A faint light flickered in her eyes. "Then you two have read my letters?"

Mac felt as cold as the snow piled outside the window. "No. We've not read them. But Oscar told us that our names were mentioned. That's how I came to be here. We figured it had to be you."

Her head bent forward, and as Mac watched her bring her hand up to her eyes, he told himself if she cried he wouldn't allow her tears to get to him. No. As a child he'd cried plenty of his own, but she'd never been around to console him or his little brother.

"I can't imagine what you must be thinking now. I—"

The remainder of her words was cut off

with a racking cough, reminding Mac of her fragile health. He didn't want the woman to be ill. Nor did he want to cause her emotional pain. He honestly didn't know what he wanted. He felt dead inside.

After the coughing stopped, she regained her breath, then looked up at him. Clearly, this time there was anguish in her eyes, but Mac could only guess what was causing it. If she'd suddenly developed a conscience it had taken her a hell of a time to do it.

"Whatever you're thinking, Mac, I never stopped loving you and Ripp. I never stopped wishing that you were in my life."

The cold indifference that had settled over him was scaring Mac. He had finally found his mother! She was saying a tiny portion of what he needed to hear her say. Yet it all seemed so insignificant now. Words couldn't replace years of desertion.

Not bothering to reply, he walked away from her and stood staring out the window. He should have let Ripp come here, he thought miserably. He should have let his brother try to come up with the right words to say to a mother who'd chosen to quit being their mother a long time ago.

But then, he couldn't wish that entirely,

Mac realized. Otherwise he would have never met Ileana. Never had the chance to hold her in his arms.

"I honestly don't know what to say to that," he finally spoke.

His words were met with silence, and he glanced over his shoulder to see that she'd closed her eyes and her hand was pressed to her bosom.

Concerned now, he walked back over to her. "Are you all right?"

"No," she answered faintly. "I—I'm very, very tired. If you'll excuse me, I need to get back in bed."

He needed answers. Answers that had haunted him and his brother for years. But those were apparently going to have to wait until another time.

"I'll get a nurse to come help you," he told her, then quickly left the room.

Moments later, at the nurses' station, he was relaying Frankie's need to one of the nurses, when he spotted Ileana hurrying toward him. The sight of her was like a ray of sunshine after a violent storm.

He walked to meet her, and she took him by the arm and led him toward the waiting area.

"You've already seen Frankie, haven't you?" she asked as her eyes continued to scan his strained features.

He nodded. "She's my mother, Ileana. That—that part of it wasn't much of a surprise, I guess. The evidence had already pretty much told us that. But I—" Pausing, he shook his head with dismay. "Seeing her was a surprise. I didn't expect her to still resemble the mother I remembered. I thought she'd be different somehow."

Aching to comfort him, Ileana clasped her hands around his. "How did she react?"

He shook his head again, and Ileana could see he was dazed.

"She was— Let me put it this way—she wasn't ever expecting to see me in her lifetime," he said bitterly.

"Oh, Mac," she said gently. "Did she explain anything?"

"We didn't get to that. I'd only been in the room for a few short minutes when she said she was tired and needed to go back to bed."

Ileana nodded. "I'm sure she wasn't lying about that. She's in a very weak condition, and the shock of seeing you probably drained her rather quickly."

Jerking off his hat, he raked a hand roughly

through his hair. "I'm sorry about that, Ileana. I'm sorry about a lot of things!" He slapped the hat back on his head. "I've got to get out of here," he muttered. "Maybe you'd better go check on her."

Frankie was her patient, but her first concern was Mac. "What are you going to do?"

"I'm going back to the Bar M. And I'm going to talk with my brother."

Ileana was greatly relieved to hear he was planning on going home to the ranch, but she was worried about his state of mind. For the first time in her life, she wished it wasn't imperative that she return to the clinic this afternoon. But her patients' welfare had to be considered, and they were all counting on her.

"I won't be home until late this evening," she said with a troubled frown. "Why don't you stop by the ranch house and visit with my parents or the hands in the barn? You shouldn't be alone, Mac."

His expression grave, he bent his head and brushed a kiss on her cheek. "I'll be okay, Ileana. Don't worry about me. I'll see you later."

He pulled away from her and walked briskly toward the exit. As Ileana watched him disappear beyond the revolving door, she realized that his happiness had become very important to her, even more important than her own.

Once Mac pulled onto the main highway and headed his truck toward the Bar M, he punched in Ripp's cell number and hoped his brother was available to take his call.

After three rings without an answer, Mac was about to hang up when he heard Ripp's voice.

"Hey, brother! You finally decided to call me and let me know you're still alive?"

Mac squinted at the curving highway ahead. "You have my number. You could have called."

"Yeah. Sorry, brother. I was only teasing. It's been heck around here. We've had several car accidents to work. Not to mention a rash of robberies. Plus Marti got sick with the flu, and I've been taking care of Elizabeth as much as I can while Luci tends to him."

"You don't need to apologize to me. We're brothers, remember." He swallowed as the image of their mother's frail image swam before his eyes. "Are you sitting down?"

"No. Why?"

"Maybe you ought to," he said grimly. "I just saw Frankie a few minutes ago."

There was a long pregnant pause, then Ripp asked, "And?"

"She didn't recognize me. Not until I told her my name. Guess it had been too long for her to know her own kid."

He could hear Ripp blow out a heavy breath.

"God, I can't believe you've found our mother! What did she say? Did she have any sort of explanation?"

"She knew Betty Jo had passed away. Apparently she keeps up with Goliad County news. But as for anything about her leaving the family—we didn't get to that. She's still very weak. I've had to save all that for another time."

"Oh," Ripp said with obvious disappointment. "So what are your plans now? To see her again?"

"I have to, Ripp. We can't just leave things dangling like this. I've come all this way to find her. Now we need to know why, don't we?"

"Yeah. The why is the thing that's always tormented me," Ripp huskily replied.

"Me, too." Mac let out a heavy breath. "Seeing her wasn't easy, Ripp."

"No. I don't expect it was. How did she look?"

The dead feeling that had come over him in the hospital room was now evaporating, leaving pain in its wake. "You remember that one picture we have of her? Well, she looked just like that. Beautiful—only older."

There was another long pause, and then Ripp said, "I think that's why Dad destroyed every picture he could find of her. He didn't want them around, reminding him of the beauty he'd lost."

"We lost her, too, Ripp."

"Yeah, but we kept her picture," he pointed out. "Don't forget that, Mac."

"I haven't forgotten anything, little brother."

Later that evening, long after dark, Ileana found Mac at her mother's horse barn, helping the grooms blanket the horses that had been worked earlier in the day. Once he and the other men finished the chore, Mac climbed in his truck and followed Ileana up the mountain to her house.

In the kitchen, he helped her lay out plates and utensils so they could eat the take-out meal she'd brought home with her.

"Why don't you sit and let me do this, Ileana," he said as she pulled out a container of fried chicken. "You've had a long day."

"It couldn't have been as nearly as long as yours," she said, then turning away from the cabinet, she walked over to him and placed her palms against his chest. "I've hardly been able to work due to worrying about you."

When had any woman ever worried about him or expressed their concern about him in any way? He couldn't remember a one and the fact that Ileana's thoughts were on him rather than herself totally amazed him.

Lifting his hand, he stroked his fingers through the hair at her temple. "Sweet girl, I'm not anything to worry over."

Her palms moved up and down against his chest. "That's not the way I see it."

The tenderness in her eyes, the warmth of her hands caused desire to flicker low in his belly. Groaning at the unbidden yearning, he bent his head and nuzzled a kiss against the side of her neck. The honey taste of her was more than a balm to his aching heart. It blanked his mind to everything, but her. "Do you think we could forget about eating for right now?" he murmured.

Her soft sigh skittered against his cheek as she slipped her arms up and around his neck. "We have all night," she whispered.

Chapter Eleven

The next morning Mac was still sound asleep when Ileana slipped from the bed and quickly readied herself for work. Rather than wake him, she left him a note on her pillow with a promise to call him later in the day, then quietly exited the house.

Throughout the dark drive to Ruidoso, their lovemaking of the night before rolled over and over in Ileana's mind like a sweet, but haunting, refrain. In spite of all the tenderness he'd shown her, she'd felt desperation behind his kisses, a hunger in his hands that she'd not felt before. The change in him had left her heart heavy because she knew, in his own subtle way, he was saying goodbye.

You knew that time would come, Ileana. You can't be sorry about it now. You can only be glad that you've had this much time with the man.

Ileana realized the voice inside her head was right, but that didn't make it any easier to accept the idea that he would soon be gone. Through all her lonely years, she'd never dreamed or imagined that a man as handsome, exciting and loving would ever come into her life. She didn't want to let him go. Yet she didn't have any right to ask him to stay. Their coming together had been without strings, without promises. To try to drag more from him now would be humiliating and meaningless.

A few minutes later Ileana found the halls of the hospital busy as shifts changed, medicine was dispersed and breakfasts served. She slowly made her way from patient to patient, carefully monitoring their condition and making a point to address their questions and concerns.

Purposely, Ileana saved Frankie's visit for her last stop, and as she knocked lightly, then entered the woman's room, she wondered what, if anything, the woman might bring up about Mac.

"Good morning, Frankie." Her patient's breakfast tray had already been pushed aside with two-thirds of the food gone uneaten. She looked pointedly at the tray, then to Frankie. "Aren't you hungry this morning?"

"No. I've been counting the minutes until you got here."

Ileana's brows lifted as she pulled a stethoscope from her white lab coat and reached for the blood pressure cuff hanging over the headboard of the bed. "Oh? Are you feeling worse? Coughing more?"

"My cough is better and I feel stronger." Frankie closed her eyes and pinched the bridge of her nose. "I'm just in turmoil." Groaning with anguish, she opened her eyes and looked up at Ileana. "Did you know about Mac? About his being here?"

Feeling a bit duplicitous, Ileana felt her cheeks fill with color. "Yes, I did, Frankie. He came to me several days ago and—well, he explained the situation and asked to see you. At the time I had to refuse. You were too ill for such a meeting. But now you're better."

Rising up to sitting position in the bed, Frankie looked at her, and Ileana could see haunting shadows in the woman's eyes. Fears and doubts etched every line of her face.

"I have to see him again, Ileana. Yesterday I was so shocked—but there was so much I needed to say. Wanted to say. Is he still here? Can you ask him to come see me this morning?"

With each word that passed her mouth, Frankie was growing more anxious and agitated. Ileana realized it would only cause her more stress if she tried to put the meeting off until a later date.

"Yes, he's still here. And, yes, I'll ask him to come. But first you must calm down, Frankie, or your heart is going to give you even bigger problems."

Shaking her head, Frankie bit down on her lip and turned her watery gaze toward the window. "I don't care about that. My heart's been broken for a long, long time," she said in a stricken voice.

Nearly thirty miles away, Mac was bundled in his coat, sipping coffee on Ileana's deck as he stared out at the surrounding mountains. But the beautiful scenery was not the thing on his mind.

He'd come here to Ruidoso for one thing

and one thing only. To see if Frankie Cantrell was his lost mother. He'd done that. Frankie Cantrell had once been Frankie McCleod, the woman who'd given birth to him and Ripp. So now what? There were lots of answers he still didn't have from the woman, but did he really want to stick around and try to pry them from her? What good would that do him or Ripp? All these years she'd clearly known where to find her two sons, yet she'd chosen not to. Wasn't that enough to tell him that she didn't care? That she'd never cared?

Sighing, he rose from the lawn chair and walked over to the railing that bordered the wide deck. Much of the snow had melted yesterday, and now patches of green juniper and sage dotted the slope of land running away from Ileana's house. The landscape and the climate were nothing like South Texas, and he'd not expected to like it. He'd expected to want to get his business done and get back home as quickly as possible, but Ileana had changed all of that. Now when he looked at the desert and mountains, he thought of her, and realized how hard it was going to be to leave them both.

He'd tossed the coffee dregs and was about to head back into the house when his cell phone rang. Seeing Ileana's number filled him with pleasure and concern.

"Ileana, you snuck off without waking me," he gently scolded.

"I didn't see any need to disturb you," she said in a rather hushed voice.

Picking up the cue that she couldn't talk freely, he quickly questioned, "Is anything wrong?"

"Yes and no. Can you come to the hospital right now? I'll explain everything when you get here."

His brows furrowed together. "Does this have anything to do with Frankie?"

"Everything. She's asking for you."

After nearly thirty years, she was asking for him. Bitterness, amazement and curiosity swirled and tangled inside him. "I'll be there as soon as I can," he muttered.

"You can catch me at the nurses' station," she told him, then quickly ended the call.

Thirty minutes later, his mind spinning with all sorts of questions, Mac sprinted across the hospital parking lot and into the building.

Nurse Renae Walker was on duty, and she

picked up the phone to page Ileana even before Mac came to a stop at the long desk.

"Dr. Sanders is on her way," she told Mac.

After thanking the nurse, he started toward the waiting area, but in a matter of moments Ileana caught up to him and, taking him by the hand, she pulled him over to one side of the wide corridor.

"I'm so glad that you've come," she said.

"Why wouldn't I?"

She shrugged. "I'm not sure. After seeing her yesterday you seemed so disturbed."

Disturbed was a polite way for Ileana to describe his feelings about Frankie. Just looking at the woman and hearing her voice had caused him to ache in a way he'd never ached before. "Ripp and I deserve answers. That's the only reason I'm doing this."

Ileana nodded grimly. "I understand, Mac. But she was so worked up this morning when I went in to see her that her blood pressure was sky-high. Whatever you've thought about her for all these years—well, I think you at least need to hear her out."

As Mac looked down at her, it struck him that just over a week had passed since he'd first come to Sierra General and met Ileana in this corridor. He'd summed her up as intelligent and qualified in her profession but plain and practical. He'd never expected, or even dreamed, he'd feel sexual attraction for the doctor, much less affection. Now he could only think how blind he'd been, how much he would have missed if he'd not bothered to look at the woman beneath the surface.

"Don't worry, Ileana. I plan to give her that much."

She nodded, and Mac gently brushed his knuckles against her cheek before he turned and headed to Frankie's room.

After a light knock on the door, he stepped in the small space to find his mother in the same armchair she'd been sitting in yesterday. This morning she was dressed in a frilly pink bed jacket, and her shoulder-length hair, still mostly black, was brushed loose around her face. She looked fifty instead of sixty, a fact that would be different, he figured, if she'd chosen to stay on the McCleod farm.

A wobbly smile touched her lips as he moved toward her. "Mac," she said quietly. "Thank you for coming."

His insides felt like coils tightened to near breaking point. "Ileana said you wanted to see me."

The smile on her face turned resigned.

"And you're here because of her. Well, that's all right. As long as you're here."

There was a wooden chair sitting against the wall. Mac pulled it closer to hers, and once he'd removed his hat and settled himself in the seat, he said, "To be honest with you I wasn't sure that I wanted to see you again. This isn't easy for me, and I expect it's no better for you. Yesterday you seemed pretty upset, and I don't want to be the reason to give your health a setback."

She made a weak, dismissive gesture with her hand. "We're not going to worry about my health. I'll be fine. And you're wrong about one thing. Seeing you yesterday wasn't hard. It was something I've wanted for a long, long time… To see you—and Ripp."

Shaking his head, Mac desperately tried to hold on to his emotions. "I'm sorry, Frankie, but that's hard to swallow. You knew where your sons lived. All you had to do was fly to Texas. Drive to Texas. Even pick up the phone."

Regret etched her features, and as Mac looked into her eyes he saw something that resembled fear. But what did this woman have to fear? he wondered. For years now, she'd been living an easy, pampered life.

"Every day, for the past thirty years, I've been aware of that, Mac. But things weren't all that easy. For a long time I was afraid to go back to Goliad County. And then later, after I heard that Owen had died—" She drew in a long, ragged breath, then released it. "Well, I figured you and Ripp were better off not knowing about me or what had happened. Betty Jo told me that you'd grown into fine young men and that you'd become respected deputy sheriffs. She made it sound like your lives were good, and I didn't want to mess that up for either of you."

Amazed, Mac stared at her. "Mess us up? What do you think you did when you walked out on us? Ripp and I watched the road for days and days. We kept telling each other that you'd come back, that you wouldn't really leave us behind! Thirty years after the fact is a little late to be worrying about messing up your sons' lives!"

Her eyes turned watery, and as she reached for a napkin, Mac tried to steel himself against her tears. She'd hurt him and his brother in the deepest way a parent could hurt a child. Yet it appeared she'd lost something in the process.

"Yes, I deserve your anger and more,"

she said with a sniff. "But I really did mean to come back after you, Mac. Things just got—" She looked at him, then with an anguished groan, she covered her face with her hand. "Oh, Mac, my son. My son. I never wanted you or your brother to know any of this. That's why I've stayed away all these years." She removed her hand and looked at him through a wall of tears. "But I can see that you don't understand and you need explanations."

Mac hadn't expected to feel as though his heart, his very insides were being torn out of him. But it did, and he struggled to hide the pain from his voice. "The not knowing has been hell for me and Ripp. Can you understand that?"

She nodded miserably. "Yes. But I believed that hearing disparaging things about your father would be even worse for you both."

Scooting to the edge of his seat, he leaned toward her. "Things about Dad? What things?"

Her jaw suddenly grew rigid, and he could see she was fighting to toughen her resolve. "I have no doubt that Owen was a good father to you boys. He loved you both so much. But our relationship was troubled, Mac. Owen was a hard-nosed, hard-driven man. His sons and the farm were his entire life. I was just something on the side, something to make his family complete."

"If you knew he felt that way, then why did you ever marry him?" Mac questioned.

She momentarily closed her eyes. "Because I loved him. And he wasn't that way when we first married. He was charming and affectionate. He treated me as his partner and cared about my interests and wants. But after you boys were born, he began to change and draw away from me. Planting, harvesting, paying the bills—that's all that mattered."

"We never had much money," Mac reasoned. "That's hard on a man who wants to give his family security."

She sighed. "That's true. But I wanted to help him. I wanted him to include me in his worries, his plans. I wanted him to see that I needed more in my life than feeding livestock and cleaning away the blowing grit of plowed fields. Not monetary things—I just needed him to love me."

"So instead of sticking it out with Dad and trying to make it work, you had an affair with Will Tomlin."

Horrified, she looked at him. "No! Sure,

everyone in town believed that's what was going on, but they were wrong! Will was a fine and decent man. All he did was befriend me and give me a place to stay while I tried to talk some sense into Owen. Betty Jo was pregnant, and I didn't know where else to go. I'd left the farm in desperation. I wanted to do something to wake him up, to make him see that we needed to make changes in our marriage. Owen would have nothing of it. He was convinced that I was having an affair, and he wanted a divorce."

Mac felt dead inside. All these years he'd believed his father was above reproach and that his mother was the guilty deserter. Now he had to face the fact that he'd been wrong and misguided about both of his parents.

Wiping a hand across his face, he muttered, "So you agreed to a divorce."

"No! I didn't want a divorce. I loved Owen. I went against my own parents' wishes to marry him. They wanted more for me than being the wife of a farmer. But I didn't care— all I wanted was Owen. But after ten years of marriage, he'd grown into a hard, angry man. When I told him that I wanted to come home, that I didn't want a divorce, he told me that I didn't have a choice in the matter and that if I ever tried to see you boys again he would kill me."

Stunned, Mac stared at her. "Surely you didn't think he was serious?"

She dabbed the napkin at her eyes. "I didn't want to think he would ever hurt me. But one day I got up my courage and drove out to the farm. I'd decided I was going to get you boys and run. Owen met me at the edge of the property and threatened to choke the life out of me. And if you could have seen him that day—" Pausing, she shivered as though she was reliving the moment. "I've never seen such rage or hatred on anyone's face. I didn't have any choice, Mac, but to turn around and leave."

Rising from his seat, Mac began to pace around the small, sterile room. "You could have gone to the police, through the courts," he accused. "Didn't that ever cross your mind?"

"Of course it did. All sorts of plans went through my mind. But was fighting Owen for custody going to make anything better for you boys? My reputation was already shot. The whole town considered me an adulteress. If I dragged Owen through the court system, then even more ugliness would come out. You and Ripp would have been devastated. I didn't have money or means to care for you. Besides, Owen's threats grew more and more frightening, and I realized if I didn't leave Texas entirely, he would probably take my life. So I signed the divorce papers and left."

The ache in Mac's chest was so deep that it was almost impossible for him to breathe. "How did you happen to settle here?" he asked thickly.

Frankie continued to wipe her eyes. "That happened by chance. My car broke down, and I didn't have the money to go any farther. I found a job at the racetrack and slowly began to start my life over."

"When you left Texas where were you headed? To stay with your folks?"

"I was going to California," she admitted. "But not to them. They wouldn't have welcomed me. I didn't know where I was going. I was scared, and I knew if I tried to contact you and Ripp, Owen would hunt me down." Her head was bent, and she covered her face with both hands. "When I met Lewis, my plans about California changed. I told him the whole story about my marriage. He wanted to get you boys and bring you both back here to live with us. But I knew how much you loved

Owen, and by then I figured you hated your mother. I decided you needed to be with your father and that I'd be doing you a favor to stay out of your lives."

"You never told Quint or Alexa," he accused. "Were you ashamed of me and Ripp?"

To his surprise she rose from the chair and steadied herself with a hand on one padded arm. "Never, Mac. I was ashamed of myself. Ashamed of failing my sons. But as time went on, Lewis and I decided it would be harder on Quint and Alexa to hear they had brothers in Texas but would never be able to see them."

Mac had never felt so cold, so utterly drained in his life. Everything he'd believed about his family had just been torn to shreds. Everything he'd imagined his father to be now appeared to be just a larger-than-life lie.

"Dad's been dead for over six years. Were you never going to see us? Never going to tell Quint and Alexa about their brothers?" he asked in a low, accusing voice.

"I honestly don't know, Mac. Ever since Betty Jo told me that Owen had passed away, I've been praying for the courage to face you and Ripp. But Owen discarded me as though I'd been no more to him than a broken-down tractor he no longer wanted. And after all these years I've feared that my sons would reject me, too. I guess God answered my prayers by sending you here."

Wiping a hand over his face, Mac walked back over to his chair and picked up his hat from where he'd placed it on the floor. After he'd levered it onto his head, he turned to face her.

"I'd better be going," he said in a choked voice.

To Mac's surprise, she reached out and touched his forearm. "Is that all you have to say?"

He forced his eyes to meet hers and wondered why he'd never been able to forget the image of her bending down and pressing a kiss to his cheek, of her smile as she'd called him her sweet boy.

"I wish there was something I could say to make it easier for both of us," he said in a low choked voice. "But I can't. There's nothing left in me, I guess."

Pain pinched her features. "I thought… I was hoping you could call me Mother— maybe just once."

His gaze dropped to the floor. "I'm sorry, Frankie, but I haven't had a mother since I was ten years old."

Before she could make any sort of reply, he turned and quickly left the room. Staying wouldn't have helped matters and like he'd told her, there was nothing left for him to say.

Back at the nurses' station he caught Nurse Walker's attention as she hung up the phone.

"Is Ileana still here in the hospital?" he asked.

The blond nurse shook her head. "Sorry, Mr. McCleod. She had an emergency at her clinic. I'm sure you can find her there."

"Yeah. Thanks."

Numbly, Mac walked out of the hospital and climbed into his truck. But once he was sitting behind the wheel, he didn't make a move to start the engine. Instead he sat staring out the windshield trying to make sense of all the things Frankie had told him.

Owen had been a hard-driven man. Mac and his brother had always understood that much about their father. But had he really been the insensitive brute that she'd described? How could the man he'd admired and loved, the man who'd spent fifteen years protecting the citizens of Goliad County, threaten to kill his own wife? If Frankie's story was true, Owen had been too stubborn and selfish to try to mend his family back to-gether. He'd deliberately kept the mother of his children away from her sons.

Oh, God, nothing was ever going to be the same, Mac thought miserably. Everything he'd ever believed in was shattered in pieces at his feet. Who the hell was he? He'd thought he was the son of a tough sheriff, who'd been loved and admired by everyone. But no one, not even his own sons, had known the real Owen McCleod.

There was no way in hell he could relay this news to Ripp over the phone. Whether he was ready or not, he had to go back to Texas and face Ripp with the truth, or at least the truth as Frankie had told it.

Closing his eyes, Mac rested his forehead against the steering wheel. He was going to have to say goodbye to Ileana, and he didn't know where he was going to find the strength.

Ileana's day was so chock-full of patients, she hardly had time to swallow a bite of her sandwich, much less take a minute to call Mac. Renae had sent her a message from the hospital that he'd asked for her, but he'd not shown up at the clinic. Nor had he called.

Now as she headed her old truck across

Bar M land, she wondered what had taken place between him and his mother. Had he gotten his answers and was his time here in New Mexico over? Just asking herself the last question sliced her with pain.

She'd passed over the bridge crossing the Hondo and was flying on up the road past the main ranch house when she spotted Mac's black truck parked in front of the pink stucco.

Slamming on the brakes, she turned the truck around in the middle of the road and headed it up the long drive to her parents' home.

When she entered the house through the kitchen, Cesar was at the gas range stirring a pot of pasta.

She walked over and kissed his leathery cheek. "Supper isn't ready yet?"

"Nobody is here, except me and Mac. Wyatt and Chloe went to some kind of drilling conference in El Paso. They won't be back for a couple of days."

"Oh. I wasn't aware that they were leaving." Usually her parents informed her if they were going out of town, but she'd been so involved with Mac for the past few days, she might have missed their call.

"It was a last-minute thing," Cesar explained, then gestured toward the sauce he was stirring. "You going to stay and have some of this?"

"I'm not sure. I need to speak with Mac first."

She left the kitchen and walked out to the living room. When she found it empty, she decided to try the room he'd been using before he'd been stranded at her house.

After knocking lightly on the door, she called his name. "Mac? Are you in there?"

He opened the door almost immediately. "Ileana. I wasn't expecting you to stop by the ranch house."

"I saw your truck parked out front," she explained, then her brow quickly furrowed in confusion. "Why are you here?"

He opened the door wider and gestured for her to enter the room. The moment Ileana stepped inside, she spotted his open bags lying on the bed.

"You're packing?" she asked incredulously. "You're not leaving tonight, are you?"

He looked at her, and Ileana could clearly feel the misery on his face. It matched the horrible pain slicing through her chest.

"Yes," he said flatly. "I don't see any point in putting it off."

Behind her back, her hands gripped tightly together as she watched him walk over to the bed and begin to stuff the remaining clothes in one of the duffel bags.

"I expected you to be leaving soon, but I—" Her throat began to ache so badly she had to stop and swallow before she could go on. "I didn't think it would be tonight."

He stared down at the bag. "I wasn't planning to leave like this, Ileana, but… Well, after this morning I have to."

Hearing the pain in his voice, she hurried over to him and placed her hand on his arm. "What happened, Mac? I was so swamped with patients today I couldn't call. I've been so worried."

He looked at her. "You didn't see Frankie this evening?"

"No. Dr. Vickers made my hospital rounds for me. What happened when you went to see her?"

A long breath rushed out of him. "She gave me the details of what happened all those years ago."

"And you believed her?"

"I have to," he said grimly. "She has no reason to lie about it now. And when a good lawman hears the truth, he usually knows it."

Ileana waited for him to explain more and just when she'd decided he wasn't going to share anything with her, he spoke again.

"My mother wanted to come home. Dad wouldn't let her. He threatened to kill her if she ever tried to get near her sons."

Ileana gasped. Even though she'd always suspected that it must have taken something dire for Frankie to leave her sons, hearing it spoken out loud was shocking.

"I guess that must have knocked your feet out from under you," she said quietly.

Leaning his head back, he stared helplessly at the ceiling. "I don't know who or what I am anymore, Ileana. My childhood, my young adult life was shaped by a man I didn't know."

"Do you think he really would have been capable of hurting Frankie?"

He dropped his head and shook it back and forth. "At first I didn't want to think so. But now that I've had a bit of time to mull it over, I have to admit that he was capable. He seemed to have an obsessive love/hate for Frankie. He forbade us boys to talk about her. Other than the one Ripp and me hid, he destroyed every photo of her in the house. And after she left the farm, he never looked at another woman."

Ileana shook her head in dismay. "Oh, Mac, I'm so, so sorry. I wish none of this had ever happened to you."

His features softened, and he sadly touched a hand to her face. "At least, out of all this, I got to know you, Ileana."

Tears were suddenly burning her throat and the back of her eyes. "Do you really mean that?"

A wry smile twisted his lips. "I've never meant anything more. Our time together has meant everything to me, Ileana. Everything."

Feeling as though she was dying right before his eyes, she turned her back to him and fought to pull herself together. She'd known all along that his time here would be brief. She'd understood that their affair could only be short-lived. She'd chosen to grab what happiness she could, for however long she could. It was now over, and she couldn't get all clingy and embarrassingly weepy.

"Will I…ever see you again, Mac?"

He was silent for a long time, and while she waited, the urge to turn and fling her arms around his neck was so great that she prayed to God to give her strength to keep from sobbing, begging him to stay.

"That's hard to say, Ileana. Maybe. Someday."

Summoning up all the courage she could find, she turned and gave him a wobbly smile. "Well, if you ever get sick and need a doctor, you know where to find one."

He looked miserable, and she was certain her heart was cracking right down the middle. Quickly, before he could make any sort of reply, she rose on her toes and pressed a kiss on his cheek.

"Goodbye, Mac. Travel safely," she whispered, then fled from the room before he could see her tears begin to fall.

Chapter Twelve

A month later, as Mac drove home from work, he glanced down at the badge on his chest and wondered why he had the urge to rip the piece of silver off his shirt and toss it out the window.

This wasn't like him. He'd always been proud of his job. He'd always felt it was his purpose in life. But ever since he'd returned from New Mexico, he'd felt little joy in anything.

His father had been an admired sheriff, who'd been elected term after term. Mac had always wanted to follow in Owen's footsteps, to be just as tough and fearless as he'd been.

But finding Frankie had changed all that. Now he kept asking himself if he was too much like his father, too obstinate and self-ish to ever have a lasting relationship with any woman.

Who the hell was he kidding? He wasn't thinking about a relationship with just any woman. He was thinking about Ileana. That's all he'd been thinking about these past four weeks. Walking away from her had been like slicing off his arms, leaving him incapable of reaching for any sort of happiness.

He was losing a battle to push Ileana from his mind, when he turned down the drive to his house and spotted his brother's truck parked near the front gate. Ripp lived thirty miles away. Unless he was here on sheriff's business, it wasn't like him to be out at night and away from his wife and children.

After parking and hurrying into the house, Mac found his younger brother in the kitchen making a pot of coffee.

"What the hell are you doing here? What's happened?" Mac blurted out.

Ripp sauntered over to the cabinet and pulled down two cups. "Nothing's hap-pened. I've just brought you something to eat, that's all."

Slightly relieved, Mac pulled off his hat and began to unbuckle the holstered pistol from his waist. "I usually manage to eat without you driving thirty miles in the dark to feed me."

"That's what I was thinking, too. But Margie says you haven't been going by the Cattle Call, so that tells me you're not eating."

Ripp carried two plates over to a small round table and tossed two forks next to them. "Lucita made a batch of tamales. She thought you might like some, and it was going to disappoint her if I didn't bring them to you. She's worried that we hardly ever hear from you."

Mac washed his hands at the kitchen sink, then grabbed a bottle of beer from the refrigerator. As he twisted off the lid, he looked at his brother. "This sudden concern for me is touching, but I don't get it. There's nothing wrong. If you'd bothered to pick up the phone and call me, I could have told you that and saved you a trip over here."

Ripp frowned. "Damn it, Mac, don't give me that crap. I've called you several times since you've gotten back from New Mexico, and each time you end the conversation before I ever get started."

"I never was much of a phone talker."

Leaning his head back, Ripp chuckled with disbelief. "You, not a phone talker? God, you are messed up."

Mac bit back a sigh. "Ripp, I'm perfectly okay."

"That's not what Sheriff Nichols says."

Mac lowered the beer bottle from his mouth. "You've talked to him about me? You went behind my back?"

Ripp went over to the microwave and pulled out a plate of tamales. "Before you get on your high horse, I didn't do anything behind your back. Sheriff Nichols called me. He's worried about you."

Stunned now, Mac walked over and flopped into one of the dining chairs. "I haven't made any mistakes on the job."

Ripp pulled out a chair and joined his brother at the table. "He never said you did. You're usually the life of the party, Mac. But the whole sheriff's department can see that you're miserable. They don't understand what's happened, and they're concerned."

A curse was on the tip of Mac's tongue, but at the last second he pulled it back. Ripp was right. He wasn't behaving like himself, and it was wrong to be lashing out at his brother.

Propping his elbows on the table, he

dropped his head in his hands. "Sorry, Ripp. I know I've been acting like a miserable bastard. I guess that's because I am."

"Why?"

Mac's head jerked up and he stared absurdly at his brother. "Hell, Ripp, do you have to ask? I've repeated every word to you that Frankie said. Does it make you happy to know that our father was a liar? That he was threatening and abusive?"

Ripp leaned casually back in his chair, and Mac could only wonder how his brother could be so calm and sensible about the whole thing. Even when he'd first come home and given Ripp the news about Frankie and her reasons for leaving, his brother had taken it all in stride.

"Not particularly. But I've come to realize that Dad wasn't a superhero. He was just a man with faults."

"He led us to believe our mother didn't want us."

Ripp nodded. "Yeah. That was wrong. Really wrong. But on the other hand, he loved us and devoted his life to raising us. I'd rather look at his good points than dwell on the bad." Ladling a couple of tamales on his plate, he glanced pointedly at Mac. "But I don't think this stuff about our parents is the thing that's really bothering you. I think something happened to you while you were in New Mexico. Something that's changed you."

Damn it, why was his brother so good at seeing through him? Or had his time with Ileana changed him so much that it showed on the outside?

Trying to make his face a blank mask, Mac tilted the beer to his lips. After downing several swallows, he said, "I found our mother, Ripp. A mother we've not seen in thirty years. Isn't that enough to change a man?"

"I would hope so."

"What does that mean?" he asked dourly.

Picking up his fork, Ripp whacked off a bite of tamale. "It means that you should be feeling better about everything. Hell, Mac, we went for nearly thirty years not knowing whether our mother was alive or dead. You found her. She's alive and she still loves us."

Mac's jaw tightened on Ripp's last words. "How do you know that? You're not the one who faced her! I was! You don't know how the woman feels about us."

Ripp helplessly shook his head. "Lucita and I have plans to visit her in a couple weeks."

Mac looked at him in surprise. "You're going to see her?"

"Of course. She's our mother, and no matter what she's done, nothing will change that." Ripp's gaze leveled pointedly at his brother. "Look, Mac, you need to stop and realize that both our parents made mistakes—stupid mistakes. But they both loved us in their own way. If you can't understand that—if you can't forgive them—then you're never going to be happy about anyone or anything."

Mac's gaze dropped sullenly to his plate. "Dad's gone. I can't talk to him about any of this."

"No. But Frankie is alive and she still matters."

Mac's fingers gripped the neck of the beer bottle. "What makes you think I haven't forgiven her?"

Ripp didn't immediately reply, and Mac looked up to see his brother thoughtfully studying him.

"Have you?" Ripp asked.

"I guess not," Mac admitted with a guilty grimace.

"Don't you think it's about time you made another trip back to New Mexico? Besides seeing our mother, I think there's someone else there who you need to see."

Mac's eyes opened wide. "Why do you say that?"

Ripp chuckled. "You figure it out, big brother."

A week earlier in Ruidoso, Ileana was in her clinic, going over important test results of a ten-year-old patient. The results had turned out to be wonderful news. The child didn't have leukemia as she'd first feared but a simple infection that had altered his blood count. Ileana was greatly relieved. Yet even this little miracle was not enough to push the heavy weight from her heart.

Nearly a month had passed since she'd told Mac goodbye. She'd not heard one word from him since then. But then she'd not expected to. She'd somehow known that once he returned to Texas he would be out of her life for good. Yet even knowing this, her heart still went into overdrive each time her phone rang. And each time it wasn't him on the other end of the line, her heart sank just that much lower.

For those brief few days in February, Mac had changed her life, and deep down she wanted to believe that she'd changed his. With each day that passed, she hoped and prayed that he would come to realize that he cared for her, that he didn't want to live without her. Yet she also realized that was romantic fantasy. Mac was back in his world, a world that she had no part in.

Ileana's miserable thoughts were suddenly interrupted when a light knock sounded on the door and her mother stepped into the room. She was carrying a white paper sack and, guessing from the odor emanating from it, Chloe had just stopped by a local fast-food restaurant.

"Hi, honey," she greeted her with a smile. "Got time for a little lunch?"

Ileana rose from the desk chair and crossed the floor to plant a kiss on her mother's cheek.

"I suppose I could stop for a few minutes. What do you have in the sack?"

"Hamburgers and French fries, what else?" Chloe said with a laugh. "And don't start preaching about the fat and cholesterol. A person has to cheat once in a while."

Smiling wanly, Ileana pulled up a chair to the front of the desk for her mother to use, then followed it with one for herself.

"Okay, I won't scold you today. I'm all out

of scoldings anyway. I've seen some very self-negligent patients this morning. They won't do a single thing to improve their health."

Chloe pulled one of the wrapped burgers from the paper sack and handed it to Ileana. "Hmm. Maybe it's a case of monkey see, monkey do."

Ileana took a seat next to her mother. "You're going to have to decipher that for me, Mother."

"That doesn't need explaining. Your patients can see that their own doctor isn't doing anything to improve her health, so why should they bother?"

Rolling her eyes, Ileana shook her head. "Mother, what are you doing in town, anyway? I thought you were taking that mare up to Santa Fe for breeding today?"

"That's tomorrow. I had a few errands to run today. One of them being you."

"Me?"

"That's right. And don't change the subject on me. Why aren't you doing anything to improve your health? A good doctor like you should know better."

Frowning, Ileana bit into the sandwich and began to chew. Chloe groaned with frustration.

"Know better than what?" Ileana asked after she'd swallowed. "I'm perfectly fine."

"Sure you are. You've only fallen into a pit of depression. You've lost weight and your eyes are circled. The few times you've stopped by the house, you say three or four words then leave. I've never seen you like this, and it worries your father and me. It especially worries us because you're not trying to do one damned thing about it."

Ileana sighed. "Mother, I told you I wouldn't scold you, so why are you doing this to me? I've already had a heck of a day. Are you trying to ruin what's left of it?"

"I'm trying to open your eyes, Ivy. You're miserable, and it's high time you do something about it."

Ileana looked down at the burger in her hands. Food was not what she wanted. She didn't want anything, except Mac. To see his face, hear his voice. "There's nothing I can do about it, Mother," she mumbled. "I simply need time."

"Time? For what?"

Ileana glanced over at her mother. The expression on Chloe's face was more than impatient; it was fed up.

"To gather myself together," Ileana answered lamely. "Can't you understand that?"

"Frankly, no. Since Mac went back to Texas you've become a zombie, and I can't see time making anything better."

Plopping the burger down, Ileana rose to her feet and began to walk aimlessly about the room. There wasn't any use in denying her mother's words. It would be silly of her to try to pretend that Mac's leaving hadn't devastated her.

"Mother, Mac has gone home to his life in Texas. His life never was here with me."

"Do you want it to be?"

Pausing in front of the bay window, Ileana looked at her with faint surprise. "I've never let myself think that far," she said in a strained voice. "It was always obvious that he wasn't serious about me, but I fell in love with him in spite of knowing that. What I want doesn't factor into anything."

Rising from her seat, Chloe walked over and gripped Ileana by the shoulders. "What *you* want should factor into *everything,* Ivy! If you love the man, you don't just sit back and wish and wonder and hope that things were different. You've got to take action."

"Action?" Ileana repeated in a dazed voice.

"Yes! Like going to Texas and telling Mac exactly how you feel. Because I have a terrible feeling that you let him go without saying one word about loving him."

Ileana's face turned beet red. "Dear Lord, Mother, how could I have mentioned the word *love* to the man? We hadn't known each other long enough!"

"You knew him long enough to fall in love with him, didn't you?"

Ignoring that question, Ileana countered, "He didn't want to hear anything like that from me. Mac is— He's a true bachelor."

"Your father believed he was a true bachelor, too. Until he met me," Chloe pointed out, then with an understanding smile, she cupped her palm alongside Ileana's face. "Darling, for years now I've watched you stand in the shadows, believing that no worthy man could ever want you. When Mac come along, I was so happy to finally see my lovely daughter come alive. You deserve to be happy, Ileana."

Tears suddenly filled Ileana's eyes. "Oh, Mom, what—what if I go to him and he doesn't care? What if he's just not interested?"

Chloe gave her an encouraging smile. "Then he's not the man you believed he was and you'll find the strength to move on. But asking yourself what-ifs isn't going to solve anything."

Hope tried to flicker in Ileana's heart as she hugged her mother close. "I'll call Dr. Nichols and see if he can run the clinic for a few days."

Two days after Ripp's late-night visit, Mac tossed a suitcase onto his bed and blindly began to toss in underwear and shirts. The afternoon was already growing late and he'd planned to leave for New Mexico this morning, but an emergency had forced him to change his plans. Several days of rain had flooded the Bianco Creek and Mac, along with several other deputies, had been called out to keep the highway clear of traffic, while ranchers drove their cattle to higher ground.

At least the task had gone off without a hitch and he'd even managed to talk Randal into filling in for him for a few extra days. And he just might need it, Mac thought grimly. Once he got to the Bar M, he had no idea how Ileana was going to greet him. These past few weeks since he'd been back in Texas, he'd not heard a word from her.

Hell, Mac, did you really think a woman like her would stop to give a guy like you a

*second thought? You're just a simple county
deputy. Do you think she'll even give a damn
when you show back up on her doorstep?*

Yes, he shouted back to the nagging voice
in his head. Ileana wasn't a snob. Her wealth
didn't determine her friends or the life she
led. So what if she hadn't told him that she
loved him. She'd given him the most private
part of herself—something she'd never done
with any man before. That had to mean something.

And you never told her you love her, Mac.

Pausing, Mac took a moment from his
packing to look around him. For years he'd
told himself that this old ranch house and the
few cattle he owned were all that he wanted.
He'd convinced himself that being a deputy
was enough to make his life feel purposeful.
And maybe it had been. On the surface he'd
been happy enough. But meeting Ileana had
changed all that.

Yes, finding his mother had shaken his
foundation and made him realize things about
his life that he'd not understood before. But Ileana was the one who'd filled his heart, who'd
made him see what loving really meant. He
didn't know why he'd not recognized how
much he loved her before he'd left the Bar

M. Walking away from her had been painful, but the empty days afterward had opened his eyes like nothing else ever had. Now he could only hope and pray that he meant something to her, something more than a bed partner.

He carried the two duffel bags into the living room and dropped them near the door, then walked back to the kitchen to make sure all the small appliances were turned off. He was giving the room one last inspection when he heard someone knocking.

Frowning at the interruption, he hurried through the house while wondering who could be showing up at his door in the middle of the afternoon. If he were needed back at the department, his coworkers would call. Ripp and Lucita had left for Fort Worth to purchase a horse for Mingo's birthday, so it couldn't be his brother showing up with another basket of food.

Running a hand through his hair, Mac pulled the wooden door open and was instantly stunned to see Ileana standing on the other side of the threshold.

She was wearing a springtime dress of blue and white flowers that showed off her waist and fluttered at her knees. Her cheeks were flushed, and her long auburn hair was flying in the breeze and teasing her face. As Mac looked at her, he was certain he'd never seen anything more beautiful than she was at that moment.

"Ileana! What are you doing here?"

A hesitant smile plucked at the corners of her pink lips. "I've been waiting for a Texan to show up on my doorstep. When he didn't, I thought I'd better show up on his."

Dazed, his heart pounding, he pushed the door wider. "How did you find this place?"

She stepped past him and into the house. Still stunned, Mac automatically closed the door, then turned to face her.

"I called the sheriff's office," she answered. "They were very helpful about giving me directions."

He watched her glance around the room, and as she did, she spotted the bags sitting a few steps away.

"Oh? Are you going somewhere?" she asked in an awkward rush. "I realize I should have called, but I wanted to surprise you."

Mac could only look at her in amazement, and then he began to laugh with more joy than he'd ever felt in his life.

"I'm sorry, Mac," she said with a pained

expression. "I guess this…my coming here was a bad idea."

Seeing that she'd totally misunderstood his reaction, he reached for her. "Oh, Ileana! It was a wonderful idea! I'm laughing because—" He pulled her closer into the circle of his arms and buried his face in her hair. "When you knocked I was about to walk out the door. I was going to the Bar M to see you."

Levering herself away from his chest, she stared up at him in disbelief. "You were coming to see me?"

Mac nodded as hope began to surge inside him. "Yes. I was hoping— Well, I planned to— Oh, hell, Ileana, I can't talk straight. I don't know how else to say it. I love you. I've been miserable without you."

Tears filled her eyes and rolled onto her cheeks. "Mac. I love you, too. I should have told you that before you left the Bar M. But I was afraid you didn't want to hear me say anything like that." Her eyes dropped to the middle of his chest. "I've been humiliated in the past, Mac. I guess I took it for granted that you would put me off, too."

Suddenly love began to fill every crack and scar in his heart, to warm each cold, empty spot inside him. "Ileana, Ileana." His hands delved into her hair, then drew her face up to his. "I couldn't say anything before now. Because I don't think I understood how I really felt about you until I got back here and took a long look at my life. It was empty—so, so empty without you."

More tears flowed down her cheeks, and he awkwardly wiped them away with his fingertips. "Will you marry me, Ileana? I realize our homes are far apart, but I can find a job in New Mexico—"

Her forefinger suddenly pressed against his lips to stop his words. "Does that really matter, Mac?"

A wide smile spread across his face. "No. Nothing matters except that we're together."

She brought her lips up to his and after a long, promising kiss, she said, "I've always wanted to live where palm trees grow."

With a finger under her chin, his doubtful gaze met hers. "But your clinic, Ileana, and your beautiful house and—"

"There are other doctors just ready and waiting to run my clinic for me. As for my house, I'm thinking it would be great for a summer vacation place." Turning in his arms, she gestured to the living room they were standing in. The furnishings didn't match, the flooring was old and the windows were bare, but to Ileana it was the most beautiful place she'd ever seen. "This house is where we need to raise our children. This little ranch will be our home."

With his hands on her shoulders, he gently turned her back to face him. "But, darling, what about you being a doctor?"

Happiness bubbled inside Ileana, and for the first time in her life she knew she could dance and laugh and shout. The same way her mother did when one of her Thoroughbreds was first to fly across the finish line.

"I've been a doctor, Mac. Now it's time for me to be a wife. A mother. A lover."

He studied her and then a smile crept across his face. "In that order?" he teased.

Rising on tiptoes, she brought her lips up to his. "Maybe we could switch them around—just for tonight," she whispered suggestively.

With a soft chuckle, he brought his arms around her. "This is one time I'm happy to follow the doctor's orders."

Epilogue

Two months later, on a bright spring day, Ileana and Mac entered Sierra General and rode the elevator up to the surgery wing. While they waited for the cubicle to stop and the doors to swish open, Ileana squeezed her husband's hand.

"Your mother is going to love the roses."

Mac glanced down at the basket of yellow roses cradled in his right arm. He'd particularly chosen the flowers because they'd reminded him of the yellow roses his mother had once grown long ago on the McCleod farm. He doubted she would make the connection, but that no longer mattered to Mac.

He'd forgiven Frankie, and their relationship was growing stronger and deeper every day.

Oddly enough, after Frankie's secret life was out and her four children were finally together, they'd been able to persuade her to have the heart surgery that she'd needed for so long. The procedure had been a complete success, and Frankie would be able to go home to the Chaparral Ranch tomorrow.

"I hope the roses cheer her," Mac said.

Ileana's eyes glowed warmly as she looked up at him. "Seeing you will cheer her, Mac. Now that I've seen you two together, I get the feeling that you were especially close to each other."

Smiling wryly, Mac said, "Ripp was always a daddy's boy. Before she left, I spent a lot of time with Mother. I guess that's why it was much harder for me to forgive and forget."

The doors to the elevator slid open, and as they automatically stepped forward, Ileana curled her arm around the back of his waist. "She's going to be just fine now, Mac. And you'll have many years to be with her. In fact," she added as they strolled down the corridor toward Frankie's room, "I was thinking it might be nice to have her come to Texas for a visit soon. We have plenty of room... for now."

Stopping in the middle of the hallway, he looked at her with an odd little frown. "What do you mean...for now? Are you trying to tell me—?"

A coy smile touched her lips. "Maybe."

"Maybe?" He looked incredulous and hopeful at the same time. "For God's sake, Ileana, you're a doctor! You should know!"

An impish smile dimpled her cheeks. "Okay, darling. I'm trying to tell you that I'm pregnant. I was going to wait until tonight when we were alone, but—" She gestured to the sterile walls around them. "We first met in this hospital, so I guess it's a fitting place to tell you that you're going to be a father."

He shook his head in happy amazement. "A father!" he softly exclaimed. "Me, a father!"

Love glowed in her blue eyes as she watched a myriad of emotions cross his face. "Does that frighten you?"

Curling his free arm around her shoulders, he pulled her close against him. "Maybe it should. But it doesn't. See, I've already learned everything not to do. And I'm going to love you and this baby, and hopefully more babies, for the rest of my life."

Bending his head, he kissed her until both of them nearly forgot that they were standing in a very public place.

Laughing, Ileana grabbed him by the hand and hurried him toward Frankie's room. "We'll take this up tonight," she promised. "Right now, let's go give your mother our news!"

Minutes later, after Mac had given Frankie the roses and told her about the coming baby, the woman hugged them both, then dabbed at the emotional tears blurring her eyes.

"You know, Mac, when you married Ileana I lost a fine doctor. But I gained a wonderful daughter-in-law. And I couldn't be happier."

Bending his head, Mac placed a kiss on top of his mother's head. "We're all happy, Mom. And that's the way it's going to stay."

* * * * *

YES! Please send me the **Home on the Ranch Collection** in Larger Print. This collection begins with 3 FREE books and 2 FREE gifts in the first shipment. Along with my 3 free books, I'll also get the next 4 books from the Home on the Ranch Collection, in LARGER PRINT, which I may either return and owe nothing, or keep for the low price of $5.24 U.S./ $5.89 CDN each plus $2.99 for shipping and handling per shipment*. If I decide to continue, about once a month for 8 months I'll get 6 or 7 more books, but will only need to pay for 4. That means 2 or 3 books in every shipment will be FREE! If I decide to keep the entire collection, I'll have paid for only 32 books because 19 books are FREE! I understand that accepting the 3 free books and gifts places me under no obligation to buy anything. I can always return a shipment and cancel at any time. My free books and gifts are mine to keep no matter what I decide.

268 HCN 3760 468 HCN 3760

Name _____ (PLEASE PRINT)

Address _____ Apt. #

City _____ State/Prov. _____ Zip/Postal Code

Signature (if under 18, a parent or guardian must sign)

Mail to the **Reader Service**:

IN U.S.A.: P.O. Box 1867, Buffalo, NY. 14240-1867
IN CANADA: P.O. Box 609, Fort Erie, Ontario L2A 5X3

HRCBPA18

Get 4 FREE REWARDS!

We'll send you 2 FREE Books plus 2 FREE Mystery Gifts.

Harlequin® Special Edition books feature heroines finding the balance between their work life and personal life on the way to finding true love.

FREE
Value Over
$20

Get 4 FREE REWARDS!

We'll send you 2 FREE Books plus 2 FREE Mystery Gifts.

Harlequin® Romance Larger-Print books feature uplifting escapes that will warm your heart with the ultimate feel-good tales.

FREE Value Over $20

Get 4 FREE REWARDS!

We'll send you 2 FREE Books plus 2 FREE Mystery Gifts.

FREE Value Over $20

Both the **Romance** and **Suspense** collections feature compelling novels written by many of today's best-selling authors.